E V E R Y T H I N G   T O   B E   E N D U R E D

R. K. MEINERS

EVERYTHING
TO BE
ENDURED

AN ESSAY ON ROBERT LOWELL
AND MODERN POETRY

A LITERARY FRONTIERS EDITION
UNIVERSITY OF MISSOURI PRESS
COLUMBIA

ACKNOWLEDGMENTS

I have incurred more obligations in thinking about the subject of this essay and in writing it than its brevity might seem to warrant. I wish to thank those friends who read all or parts of earlier versions—particularly Howard Fulweiler, Larry Vonalt, and Donald Yeats. I wish to thank Owen Barfield for reading the manuscript and for allowing me to attend his seminar on Coleridge. The dedication records my deepest gratitude: to the memory of a good friend and extraordinary man, and to my wife for bearing with me—not only through the writing, but through everything prior to the writing.

I wish to thank the publishers and authors who have granted permission to quote from the following materials:

Quotations from "Christmas in Black Rock," "The Quaker Graveyard in Nantucket," and "The Slough of Despond" from Robert Lowell's *Lord Weary's Castle* are used by permission of Harcourt, Brace & World, Inc.

Quotations are reprinted with the permission of Farrar, Straus & Giroux, Inc., from three titles by Robert Lowell: *Life Studies*, copyright © 1956, 1958, 1959 by Robert Lowell; *For the Union Dead*, copyright © 1960, 1961, 1962, 1964 by Robert Lowell; *Near the Ocean*, copyright © 1963, 1965, 1966, 1967 by Robert Lowell. The stanza from "Near the Ocean," originally published in *The New York Review of Books*, is quoted by permission of Robert Lowell.

Quotations from *Poems (1960)*, by Allen Tate, are used by permission of Charles Scribner's Sons. The quotation from "The Maimed Man," originally published in *The Partisan Review*, is used by permission of Allen Tate.

Quotations from *The Collected Poems of Wallace Stevens* are used by permission of Alfred A. Knopf, Inc.

TO THE MEMORY
OF ALAN SWALLOW
AND FOR LYNN

IN the famous Preface of 1853, Matthew Arnold explained why he was omitting "Empedocles on Etna" from this edition of his poems. It was true, he admitted, that his protagonist suffered from peculiarly "modern" frustrations, but this was not a sufficient reason for preserving the poem. There is a strangely contemporary resonance in Arnold's language. He might almost be observed in the act of anticipating Wallace Stevens, for Arnold remarks that in the person of Empedocles "the dialogue of the mind with itself has commenced." Had we not read "Empedocles on Etna," it would not astonish us if that suppressed work were in fact found to contain something akin to Stevens' best nineteenth-century-meditative style, and to learn that it had been rejected because of its hyperbolic *self*-consciousness:

> It has to be on that stage
> And, like an insatiable actor, slowly and
> With meditation, speak words that in the ear,
> In the delicatest ear of the mind, repeat,
> Exactly, that which it wants to hear, at the sound
> Of which, an invisible audience listens,
> Not to the play, but to itself, expressed
> In an emotion as of two people, as of two
> Emotions becoming one.
> (Stevens, "Of Modern Poetry")

But Arnold could not find the desire, and perhaps not the courage, to write poetry in that vein which has become so very recognizably modern; the "poem of the act of the mind" was singularly unappealing to him:

> But the modern critic not only permits a false
> practice; he absolutely prescribes false aims.—'A

1

true allegory of the state of one's own mind in a representative history,' the Poet is told, 'is perhaps the highest thing that one can attempt in the way of poetry.' [Arnold is quoting a contemporary reviewer in the *North British Review*.]—And accordingly he attempts it. An allegory of the state of one's own mind, the highest problem of an art which imitates actions! No, assuredly, it is not, it never can be so: no great poetical work has ever been produced with such an aim.

Perhaps it will not be too unfair to Arnold to see him with these words declining the gambit of modern aesthetics and the risk of modern poetry. He refuses to venture into the realms of what Yvor Winters later was to call "expressive form," as he abjures the burden of romantic self-consciousness and the philosophy of the participative and creative intelligence. But Arnold did not take the step in the kind of ignorance that has occasionally been ascribed to him. For at the same time that he refused to become a "modern" poet (in one of the senses we all recognize and with which I shall be concerned), he provides us with, to use his own word, one of the earliest conscious "touchstones" of the modern sensibility:

> What then are the situations, from the representation of which, though accurate, no poetical enjoyment can be derived? They are those in which the suffering finds no vent in action; in which a continuous state of mental distress is prolonged, unrelieved by incident, hope, or resistance; in which there is everything to be endured, nothing to be done. In such situations there is inevitably something morbid, in the description of them something monotonous. When they occur in actual life they are painful, not tragic; the representation of them in poetry is painful also.

The contemporary ear may wince at Arnold's diction.

"Poetical enjoyment" has a naive and boyish ring to it, and how out of place it would sound in most of *our* discussions of poetry; it is as if we had ruled quite out of our consciousness and even our history any memory of the Horatian dictum: *Aut prodesse aut delectare.* We have come to expect, and even to demand, in our poetry the "painful" representations Arnold decried.

With what may appear an enviable confidence, Arnold turned from the poetry of passive suffering and called for a poetry that would return to the proper, the "eternal" objects of poetry: the representation of human action and, preferably, action of heroic dimensions. He would allow the "lyric" poem to remain for the poet who *must* be subjective (he mentions the "lyric" again in the brief Preface of 1854); but of course the word "lyric" loses all meaning in the nineteenth century as *all* poetry moves away from the imitative bases of classical criticism and becomes attached to immediate personal experience. Certainly Arnold the poet knew what Arnold the critic did not, and he wrote very little poetry during the rest of his life. And what he attempted to write in accordance with the principles of his own Preface was mostly bad. Arnold surely knew, at least in private, that it was no longer possible to separate the arena of experience into those neat compartments, active and passive, and that even a poetry that found a "vent in action" was no guarantee that a continuous mental distress could be avoided. Though in his later work Arnold liked to pretend that the Romantics represented a sport—an outburst of genius doomed to failure because it "did not know enough"—he must have understood that things could never again be quite the same: from now on all poetry, whether heroic or lyric, dramatic or meditative, was to be personal poetry. As a *personal* art, poetry could be imaginative and aspiring in a way perhaps not possible earlier. But art then must also partake of the essential limitations of personality, and we record the greatest of those limitations in our elementary logic lessons: all men are mortal. When the aspiration of the romantic imagination on the one hand and the facts of mortality on the other are conjoined in the same art, there is more than a possibility that the really essential quality of such art will be frustration. In poet after poet in the last two centuries we may read emblematic histories: Hölderlin, Coleridge, Baudelaire, Rimbaud, Hofmannsthal, Robinson, Crane. Poets, with other men, have always suffered frustration; but it seems safe to say that at no other period has the poet insisted so strenuously that the condition is inevitable. And in those rare and marvellous cases where we see the poet triumphing over frustration (for example, in Yeats's later poems, or in some of Delmore Schwartz's last work, or in the final portions of Roethke's "Lost Son" sequence), we are nearly always aware that it has been as the climax of the most arduous kind of process.

I have been speaking of Arnold because he so clearly provides an entrance (among many possible entrances) to the subject that Lionel Trilling has called —echoing Arnold himself—"the modern element in modern literature." I am interested in speaking of at least one strain—in my view the crucial one—in that "modernism" which is such a constant subject of discussion. It is a word that our age has stridently demanded. We have appropriated "modern" for all sorts of discussions of our peculiar spiritual conditions, and particularly for discussion of our art. The word has come to signify a nearly aggressive insistence upon how different affairs are with *us* than they were formerly. Indeed, we often forget how relatively recently the word "modern" came to acquire anything like its present significance, and how thoroughly it is tied in with the development of historical studies and clear notions of *self*-consciousness in European thought.[1] Now, of course, we are beset with knowing discussions of "modernity" in literature (the uncanny *knowledgeability* of the commentators is itself a nearly infallible symptom of the condition); and we even have anthologies devoted to *The Modern Tradition* or *Literary Modernism*.

In these circumstances I feel somewhat hesitant about going further into the discussion, about thrusting another voice into what is already a Babel of voices. Surely we have had enough talk of these matters, and of apocalypse and crisis, says one portion of my mind. Yet no one can avoid the subjects in discussing modern literature, and they are a necessary part of my own discussion.[2] In this essay I wish to speak primarily of several writers: Allen Tate and Robert Lowell, and particularly Lowell. I wish, to be sure, to

1. The *Oxford English Dictionary* will, I believe, verify this point. I am, however, indebted to Owen Barfield's *History in English Words* (Grand Rapids, 1967; first published London, 1926) for this point.

2. I wish to make it plain that it is not only for their own sakes that I am dwelling on these subjects. This essay is conceived of as part of a projected longer work that will discuss other attempts to break out of that stifling enclosure of the private personality which has been implicit in certain elements of our major intellectual traditions for at least the past three centuries. Seen in this way, T. S. Eliot's later poetry, for example, belongs to a recognizable tradition; it can well be interpreted as an attempt to find the way out of the impasse represented in "I have heard the key / Turn in the door once and turn once only / We think of the key, each in his

comment on them and their relationship to each other, but, more importantly, I wish to see them against the background of a larger tradition. I want to use them (and again, particularly Lowell) rather as Arnoldian touchstones for an essential element in this modern tradition. In fact, I hope to evoke through them an extreme statement of the conditions with which the modern poet has often seemed to have been faced, and the circumstances from which he has tried to break free. And, finally, I must admit that one reason for attempting an essay on subjects as grand and general as these is a certain dissatisfaction on my part with much recent writing in this area.

One cannot fail to admire the intelligence and devotion that have gone into many of the recent studies of modern literature, nor can one fail to learn from them. But one also cannot help but recognize a denaturing and insulating process that often seems to take place in the same criticism. It is a criticism that seems to identify and place contemporary writers even as they write, with a rapidity that would surely bemuse those polemicists of the 1930's who complained that scholars had no sense of the present moment. And it so often seems to exist at a very great distance from the literature, and from the life in the literature, and from our life. Now it is certain that no one can avoid—certainly my own discussion cannot avoid—this essential difficulty of criticism, its tendency to fall into patterns that become only too pleasing and quickly abstract, so that we can see in literature only what our

---

prison." The attempt to break through to a larger and more wholesome vision of reality characterized much of the major romantic poetry and continues to characterize the most important poetry of the twentieth century. My later work will be concerned with some attempts to achieve such a vision.

particular pattern will describe. For I, too, have chosen to speak about a representative pattern, and I have no guarantee that what I have to say will not have a similar denaturing effect. But nothing should be allowed to obscure that essential tone in modern literature that is recognizable in Arnold's 1853 Preface, that grows during the next three quarters of a century into a tone that bursts into post-1914 writing, and that can adequately be described only in the most direct, forceful terms. To be blunt, the only *real* problem of modern "aesthetics" is: is life worth living? I believe we all know this; certainly my own generation has been weaned on the knowledge. We contrive elaborate schemes for discussing our post-lapsarian knowledge, and we publish the results—assuredly for pride and professional advancement, old and honorable motives —but also in a strange spirit of exorcism: if we are knowing enough, the problems may go away. But they will not. And these elaborate techniques of exorcism and indirection that we all practice in discussing modern literature then become part of the apparatus of impersonalization; they become part of the very problems they were evolved to describe (there is no more obvious example of this process than that which is very visibly taking place in the dissemination of Mr. McLuhan's opinions and vocabulary).

Immediately on the heels of the question, is life worth living, come its corollaries: is there anyone I can talk to, or any way we can speak together? The story is told of David Hume, sitting in his study and meditating too deeply on the inevitability of solipsism, rushing out into the billiard room and the reassuring presence of friends. Presumably this course is always open to modern professors and critics when they have sunk too far into clerkly despair; and there is always

Dr. Drink and a fifth of therapy (to borrow J. V. Cunningham's figure). But, the benefits of spirits and society aside, the questions will not leave. Everyone knows these things, but we contrive to forget them. It is really neither brash nor extravagant to see Matthew Arnold, gritting his teeth and refusing to write poems of passive suffering, prophesying Albert Camus: "there is but one truly serious philosophical problem, and that is suicide." In his impatient manner Camus was correct. Anyone beyond a certain elementary degree of intellectual sophistication can poke holes in the logic of *The Myth of Sisyphus*, but he will not in the process succeed in turning the impact of that brutal main point. All the other philosophical questions and aesthetic conundrums are secondary; one must first try, as well as he can, to answer the fundamental question.

II

IN *The Winter Sea* (1944), published not quite a century after Arnold's remarks on the suffering personality and the mind's meditation upon itself, Allen Tate wrote:

> Towards nightfall when the wind
> Tries the eaves and the casements
> (A winter wind of the mind
> Long gathering its will)
> I lay the mind's contents
> Bare, as upon a table,
> And ask, in a time of war,
> Whether there is still

To a mind frivolously dull
Anything worth living for.
("Winter Mask: To the Memory
of W. B. Yeats")

It is "towards nightfall," and the "winter wind" blows; it is wartime. The personality is driven back into its house, and it examines the interior furnishings. If there is a little more vigor than one might expect from Arnold's passive sufferer, we nevertheless recognize the situation for what it is; the "dialogue of the mind with itself" has taken on the tone we all recognize. And the final question is precisely that of Camus: why live?

It will be part of my argument that Tate exemplifies, to an unusual degree, what I have called a central strain in the modern situation.[3] Tate and Robert Lowell represent two generations of American poets. Tate is a second-generation "modernist" poet, and Lowell's career moves into what has been called the "postmodern" era. Although I do not really like these adjectives—they are far too pat, and anyone can easily question them—they ought to be sufficiently clear for the moment; I shall later argue the relationship between the two more fully. I want to argue that in these two poets we have something very like an ar-

3. I have previously written extensively on Tate (*The Last Alternatives*. Denver: Alan Swallow, 1963). It may seem odd that I am writing on him again. It is not that I have nothing else to say, or that I wish to repeat or in any way defend the earlier book. I am considering Tate in this context because of my increasing conviction of his *representative* place in modern literature, an aspect of his work I slighted before, and indeed did not fully appreciate. This might not seem a sufficient reason. To it I would add that I am concerned with the relation between Tate and Lowell, and that I am really more concerned with Lowell than Tate. And, above all, I want to use their work to evoke a typical modern syndrome.

chetypal modern situation, and that this situation is characterized by a sense of the isolation of the personality so strong that it deserves to be called obsessive and claustrophobic. It is further characterized by a desperate attempt to break out of these oppressive circumstances (represented everywhere in modern writing in images of traps, mazes, dungeons, nets, caverns, locked rooms, mirrors, etc.). This attempt typically results in extremity of all sorts: violent language, unusual dramatic situations, contorted metaphors, and in general either straining or parodying all the traditional literary conventions. The ensuing struggle leads to the question of whether the struggle is, after all, worth it, in a day in which even a phrase like "the death of God" can become a platitude. Perhaps the situation is not only typically modern, but in a sense typically American. I do not intend to explore the question of the peculiar characteristics of American experience, but I might remark in passing that, if Allen Tate has reminded us that Edgar Allan Poe is his (and our) cousin, then certainly Robert Lowell is a nephew in the same family.

The archetypal "modern" situation, I have called it, which is certainly both far too simple and too general. There is literally no way short of a very large volume to document the assertion, a volume that would very likely be repetitive. As Erich Auerbach says in the closing pages of his great work, *Mimesis*, if he had attempted to write the history of European realism, the material would have swamped him. Similarly, if I were to try to demonstrate that for approximately the last two centuries an obsessive theme has been growing, and that this sense of the personality driven into a corner is what unites nearly all modern literature, it is just *barely* possible that I might escape redundance. Although the last twenty years or so have seen the production of a number of impressive works that have taught us that modern literature and culture must be seen as extensions of that remarkable evolution in human consciousness usually called romanticism,[4] there might still be room for a work that traced the romantic poet, the "single, solitary person" in two directions: toward Stevens' "figure of the youth as a virile poet" on the one hand, but toward Eliot's "hollow men" and the haunted personae of his late plays on the other hand as well. To be complete, this work should also deal with the development of romantic ideas, particularly those conceptions clustered around the nucleus of the creative and mythopoeic imagination, into something very like a new critical orthodoxy, which at the present time shows signs of dominating the academic study of not only modern literature but all literature.[5] But even if I were to escape redundance,

4. I am thinking particularly of the work of men such as Geoffrey Hartman, Louis Martz, Robert Langbaum, M. H. Abrams, Northrop Frye, Roy Harvey Pearce, Harold Bloom, and Morse Peckham—and there are many others. J. Hillis Miller obviously belongs here, too, with his valuable books on nineteenth- and twentieth-century poetry. I must, however, disagree with his contention, presented in the first chapter of *Poets of Reality*, that while modern poetry develops out of romanticism, it is not only more than an extension of romanticism, but develops into something quite different. This is not the place to quarrel with Mr. Miller, but his major thesis does not really convince me. It seems at the same time to overemphasize the "newness" of twentieth-century poetry and to underemphasize traditional elements in romanticism.

I wish to add that the highly original and provocative works of Owen Barfield have probably meant more to me in this area than those of any other writer, even when I find myself in disagreement with him.

5. There has already been a good deal of discussion that would bear on the first portion of this hypothetical work. The second portion remains to be written, and it *ought* to be writ-

I would surely be overwhelmed by examples. There are endless possibilities: Rimbaud's "le désordre de mon esprit," the mocking urbanity of Wilde and its aftermath, Hofmannsthal's Chandos letter, the preternatural sensitivity of Poe's characters, the comparable but domesticated awareness of James's people—there is no end.

Still, as Auerbach says, if one has deduced the motif correctly, then it must appear in exemplary texts. The texts I have chosen are the works of Allen Tate and Robert Lowell, and I hope to justify seeing in them something like the extreme condition with which any modern poet who has attempted to break through into a vision of freedom and wholeness must deal.

Tate's *The Winter Sea* was issued in a limited edition by the Cummington Press in 1944 (all of the poems in the volume can be found in his collected *Poems*). Anyone who has read *The Winter Sea* recognizes the fierceness and melancholy of these poems; and though these very qualities, as well as other char-

---

ten. There have, to be sure, been discussions of psychological criticism, myth criticism, archetypal criticism, and other forms of criticism labeled with tags linking them with the romantic tradition. But there is something melancholy in the spectacle of even so brilliant a writer as Northrop Frye creating a critical machinery from ideas that were originally so militantly antimechanistic. This is unjust to Frye. His splendidly witty mind keeps him from ever carrying his insights to such extremes. It is not unjust, however, to many of the host of his disciples and other laborers in the same vineyard who, under the warrant of an ill-assorted bag of ideas gathered from Frazer, Harrison, Jung, Eliade, Cassirer, Kerenyi, and a multitude of similar sources, have once more found an all-purpose tool to apply to the study of literature and culture, one that releases them from the difficulty of thinking closely about particular cases. If the second portion of this hypothetical study should ever be written, I suggest it should be divided into two sections: The Triumph of Romance, and The Arrogance of Romance.

acteristics of Tate's work, may alienate some readers, I do not think it is hard to draw the conclusion that the book was one of the most distinguished American books of the Second World War. The image of the "winter sea" was crucial. One of the book's major premises—and this applies particularly to "Seasons of the Soul," the most important poem in the book[6]— is that the "sea" itself had finally gone bad. The malaise could no longer be even symbolically localized: no more moral paralysis centered in Dublin, nor even the European tradition shattering into exquisite fragments in London. Now the very depths of life were treacherous; the ego floated precariously over hidden and shark-torn waters, and from the depths there came no potency or revivification, but the threat of mere bestiality and pointless recurrence.

Should a generation practically initiated into intellectual awareness by Freud and Nietzsche have found anything to wonder at in these possibilities? As the old moralities crumbled, new and rational moralities were to emerge, were they not? Perhaps even a postmoral era, morals bearing the taint of theologies? The gods being dead, human intelligence and imagination, finally liberated from the idols of cave and tribe, were to come forth into the sunlight, and men should see that the powers that had created the gods

6. I discussed the poems in *The Winter Sea* in my earlier book, particularly "Seasons of the Soul," which was perhaps analyzed at too great a length. The poem is certainly worth the consideration, but I must admit the justice of Edwin Muir's remark that the danger of too much analysis of this type is that the reader may very well feel that "I am being confined in a narrow place with the poem and the critic, and that I shall not get away until all three of us are exhausted" (*The Estate of Poetry*). My earlier analysis approached this work only in relation to Tate's own career.

in the first place could now proceed unaided. That was the hypothesis, advanced in many forms during the previous century. Nietzsche would have scorned such simplistic nonsense, particularly in his darker moments, but how many others have not so read Nietzsche? In Tate's poems, however, the hypothesis was certainly not operating; the human personality did not seem to be moving confidently into the future. Tate, and others like him, had failed the challenge, had suffered a "failure of nerve": that was the reaction of many reviewers. It was a case of conservative panic, in Tate's case complicated by his habitual stance: southern, patrician, aloof, and intractably melancholy.

I had hoped this overblown rhetoric might bring up to the surface of the mind the tones and conditions of two decades ago, tones that we can resurrect by leafing back through the bound volumes of literary quarterlies. I—and I suppose most people my age—couldn't really participate in the tones and conditions, being too young; but they have adopted me. If the paragraph is gauche, it is symbolically so, and I am sceptical of its ability to provoke any other reaction than that of low amusement. "Failure of nerve" is old hat. We *know* all these things. We have been there. We have not only learned to live with them, we are bored with them. We are not surprised, we will not be surprised, there is nothing that could happen that is beyond our expectation. Personal and social crises come cheap—even our own. If a friend cut his throat at the next cocktail party we would not be astonished, nor if we learned that Cincinnati had vanished last night. A lifted eyebrow, an allusion to E. M. Cioran or William Burroughs, and we are on our way once more. How can we respond to talk of a botched civilization, to quaint metaphors like "an old bitch gone in the teeth," to *la trahison des clercs* and searches for identity? These things have become the properties of naïveté; they belong to the very young with their hair, their amplifiers, converting the clichés we are bored with into electronic songs of innocence and experience (a process that would seem to vindicate Marshall McLuhan's observation about the new environment appropriating and reprocessing the old one, but that probably points at even deeper and more interesting possibilities).

Tate's book provoked a good deal of comment; the fierceness of his attitude toward contemporary American experience and America's role in the war came in for much disapproval, and many critics chided him for his low opinion of human nature. Still, the artist must be granted his *donnée*. It is one of the most revered clichés of organic aesthetics, and most of Tate's critics were willing to grant at least this much. Henry James's observation comes from the very center of the romantic syndrome: the moment of perception is sacred; the personality's authentic experience fully rendered is the most meaningful criterion of valid art. The paradox here is, the artist must be granted his *donnée* even if that *donnée* bears witness to the possible extinction of art and the personality itself. This is what was palpably taking place in Tate's poems: the ability of the personality to maintain its transactions with other persons and with the world at large was breaking down. The "time of bloody war" of "Seasons of the Soul" was not a cause, but a symptom. Man was divided against himself, and isolated from both his own past and from any refreshment in nature.

It is, in the proper sense, *terribly* difficult to write

adequate poetry of the negative vision, particularly when that vision has proceeded this far. For a poet, such as Tate, with formalist commitments, with beliefs in the traditional orders of grammar and rhetoric, this is particularly true. The logic of syntax and the absurdity of experience continually joggle each other, and any kind of equilibrium can be of only the most tenuous sort. The difficulty of the effort shows in every line of Tate's poetry. He had before been considered a poet of notably "violent" language and images, but the poetry of *The Winter Sea* shows the strain even more than the earlier work, for the elaborately formal verse is at such a great variance with the vision of the poems. If Tate's earlier poetry had been "difficult," what could be said about this verse? The wiry, Latinate, allusive poetry seemed to evoke more sorrow and crisis than it could contain, and the very tight elegance of the poetry seemed, to many readers, to tail off constantly into obscurity.

However difficult it might be to identify all the nuances of some of the passages, however, it would seem that few of the readers who constituted the audience for a limited edition by a poet with a reputation for difficulty would need much glossing to grasp the import of the lines that close "Seasons of the Soul":

> Then, mother of silences,
>
> Speak, that we may hear;
> Listen, while we confess
> That we conceal our fear;
> Regard us, while the eye
> Discerns by sight or guess
> Whether, as sheep foregather
> Upon their crooked knees,
> We have begun to die;
> Whether your kindness, mother,
> Is mother of silences.

Tate's "mother of silences" is, among other things, the dark side of Henry Adams' Virgin, the statue who stares from the grave of Adams' wife into the impenetrable mystery of the past and the future; and she is the perfect emblem of Arnold's passive sufferer locked into the present moment, aware of that moment's estrangement from past and future but unable to break out of it.

Now consider this from Robert Lowell, written a little more than twenty years later:

> Pity the planet, all joy gone
> from this sweet volcanic cone;
> peace to our children when they fall
> in small war on the heels of small
> war—until the end of time
> to police the earth, a ghost
> orbiting forever lost
> in our monotonous sublime.

This is from "Waking Early Sunday Morning," the first poem in *Near the Ocean* (New York, 1967). If there was ever any aptness (I will not say justice) in ascribing a "failure of nerve" to Tate, what shall we make of Lowell? We may well be relieved that "failure of nerve" has made its way to the limbo of slogans, for slogans never penetrate very deeply. But it is important to realize that, making due allowances for the difference in the ages of the two writers and the quite dissimilar circumstances of their literary careers, Lowell's poetry proceeds out of what is essentially the same negative vision as Tate's, one chastened by twenty more years of modern experience.

I am not claiming that the passage from Tate and that from Lowell are anything like equivalents. Lowell's verse, by this stage in his career, had become much less taut than his own earlier work; it seems to be much more relaxed than Tate's poem (it is worth noting in passing that the short rhymed lines moving in irregular metrical patterns against the tight stanzas is a point of formal similarity with the Tate poem of at least some interest). Then, too, Lowell's verse seems more directly involved with contemporary experience: Vietnam, the state of American society and experience, seem to be closer to Lowell's verse than the Second World War and contemporary American experience seemed to be to Tate's. I say "seemed" advisedly, for such experience was really a very intimate part of Tate's earlier poem. Lowell's seems far more a secular and post-Christian poetry; it is less directly modified by religious imagery than Tate's, and it does not seem to be as immediately haunted by the lost Christian order of European civilization. And, if we wish to make political analogies, it will seem to many that Lowell's is as much a poetry of the political left as Tate's was of the right. Nevertheless, in spite of the fact that we should certainly emphasize the differences between the two, we must recognize that the situations in these two poems are very close indeed. If Lowell's tone is even more sceptical than Tate's, and his resignation more profound, in both cases we are presented with the poet writing out of the sense of deep personal and historical crisis that I have been describing. I am quite aware that similar remarks could be applied to many, and perhaps most, modern poets; indeed, one might have to look hard to find a modern writer quite *without* such a sense of crisis. But I am suggesting that, quite beyond this general quality, Tate and Lowell share an uncannily similar vision, one that generates very similar tones. I am also suggesting that this negative vision might well be seen as a limiting condition, and that nowhere in modern writing is the personality driven into a much tighter corner. Not even seemingly more spectacular examples, such as Beckett or Sartre, move further into that place which is *the* condition out of which all modern literature proceeds.

It is, therefore, worth glancing at this relationship between Tate and Lowell, though I will do little more than glance at it. The relationship between the poetry of these two writers is an essential part of my subject, but it is more important to discuss the ground the two share than to spend much time arguing that they do in fact share it. It could be done, but not without one of those long and chancy discussions of influence that it would be as well to avoid here. I must spend *some* time on the matter, however, for quite apart from my larger argument, it is high time that someone had *something* to say on the relationship between the two men. The silence on this subject in the burgeoning criticism of Lowell is more than puzzling, and one looks in vain for intelligent discussions of Lowell's relation to Tate or of the resemblances between their work. Indeed, it is surprisingly difficult to find much really thoughtful consideration of the relation of Lowell to the major traditions of modern poetry.[7]

In addition to *The Winter Sea*, Tate published another piece with the Cummington Press in 1944. This

7. A great deal has been written on Lowell, of course, including several books. From my point of view, M. L. Rosenthal's opening chapter of *The New Poets* (New York, 1967), " 'Modernity' and the New Poetry" is probably more to the point than most other criticism. Mr. Rosenthal's long section on Lowell, however, is so preoccupied with the question of "confessional" poetry that he has little time for other issues. Probably the best single consideration of the question, for my purposes, is found in Thomas Parkinson's brief essay on *For the Union Dead* in *Salmagundi*, I (1966–1967), 87–95. Parkinson's essay has been reprinted in *Robert Lowell: A Collection of Critical Essays* (Englewood Cliffs, 1968), which he edited for the Twentieth

was the Preface to Robert Lowell's first book, *Land of Unlikeness*, which like Tate's volume was issued as a limited edition by Cummington. Speaking of the work of the younger writer, Tate referred to Lowell's "bold and powerful style," and remarked that the writer was "consciously a Catholic poet." Anticipating the clamorous rhetoric of Lowell's early style, Tate observed that the vehemence of this poetry was such that it seemed as if it was deliberately *willing* its Catholic imagery on a recalcitrant world, as if it could recall by main strength a vision that had all but vanished, or resurrect the image of God from the blood and machinery of the twentieth century.

Since Tate wrote, I doubt if there has been another critic of Lowell's work who has not, in one way or another, remarked the extraordinary energy of his early style. That energy, which frequently bursts out into an uncontrolled splutter, comes more under control as Lowell's writing matures; but there are few writers whose poems have so given the sense that they are held in place by main force, ready to explode at any moment. Even the quieter late poems have this quality, and there is that about their quietness which makes it frequently appear like lassitude, as though this poetry only too well remembered the early work, the poetry "of a man contracting every muscle, grinding his teeth together until his shut eyes ache," as Randall Jarrell described it. Lowell's critics, confronted with these energies, have often beat a path through literary history and many volumes of philosophy, theology, and liturgy searching for the sources of his style, or ana-

Century Views Series. This same collection also reprints Tate's preface to *Land of Unlikeness,* and the best essay on Lowell's translations I have discovered, "The Two Voices of Translation," by Donald Carne-Ross.

logues to it. In a sense, it is proper enough that they should do so and, given the critical climate that existed for the poems, it was certainly inevitable. Lowell is an historically minded poet. His work draws in intimate ways on earlier poetry. He has written "Imitations" of one sort or another throughout his career. Therefore, while I do not argue that it is useless or beside the point to look to earlier poetry when reading Lowell, I *do* suggest that to look at the past too steadfastly may be to blind oneself to what ought to be clear: the poet with whom Lowell has the closest spiritual affinity is, in a number of important ways, Allen Tate.

Everyone interested enough in Lowell to find out something about his work knows that as a young poet he was "indebted" to Tate. Nearly everyone has also let the matter rest right there, passing quickly on to other things, after perhaps noticing that one can't call a poem and a book "For the Union Dead" without bowing in the direction of Tate. What makes the situation even more strange is that Lowell himself, on several occasions, has been very open in acknowledging his early debts to Tate. But the relationship between the two men is not one that can be done justice simply by referring to influences on Lowell's youthful style— the halcyon summer spent in the tent on Tate's front lawn writing sonnets, taking dictation from Ford, imbibing formalism and Southern rhetoric. There are deep and constant kinships in their work, and these are embodied in a series of tones and attitudes that has everything to do with the typicality I am claiming to see in them.

If this were merely a matter of direct influence it would be both easier to prove and of less significance. What is easier to find than an influence? And what does it show? I could suggest to some of those critics who have roamed widely looking for analogies to Lowell's explosive language that they read carefully such of Tate's poems as "The Wolves," "The Trout Map," "Sonnets at Christmas," "Causerie," "Ditty," "Retroduction to American History," the late "The Maimed Man," and the other better-known poems, paying particular attention to recurring images. But Lowell's art isn't to be "explained" by the fact that he learned from Tate, or any other source. How could it be from any one "source" that came such features of Lowell's poetry as the persona of the tormented modern who knows more than he should and less than he needs to know? The overwhelming apocalypticism (contrary to some of his critics, it is as present in Lowell's later "secular" poetry as in the earlier "religious" poetry) isn't something one "learns" from another. Nor is that sense of the personality pushed to its last limits that constantly dominates Lowell's work. These are familiar aspects of the modernity I have evoked in the names of Arnold and Camus. But, in spite of the fact that everyone recognizes these qualities, they are brought to a peculiar and highly self-conscious intensity in Tate. Lowell shares much of the peculiarity, the intensity, and certainly the self-consciousness. This last assertion can be demonstrated only by a careful reading of the two, by a comparison of certain typical tones, situation, patterns of imagery. It is a task that would be worth undertaking, and for far more than the sake of understanding the ground the two share. That is large enough, and Lowell quietly acknowledges it in the many times his work, both early and late, either directly echoes or otherwise gestures toward Tate's poetry. But it is even more important to attempt to understand the significance of the great intensity that is generated in the work of these two writers.

III

WHERE does Robert Lowell "begin" as a poet in the early 1940's? How does one "account" for poems like "At the Indian Killer's Grave" or "Mr. Edwards and the Spider" or "Where the Rainbow Ends"? There are many possible ways, and most of them have been examined: the rebellion against the New England tradition and a sort of love/hate obsession with some of the characters of the New England past (particularly Jonathan Edwards); the poet's growing unhappiness with his city, his family, and their involvements in New England's theological and mercantile past; the seductions of Catholic ritual and thought, so shockingly "different" from the insular New England Mind; the violence of the war in Europe and of America's response.

But none of these are, I would argue, the fundamental issues. These qualities are all undeniably present in Lowell's poetry, but (and of course I am not speaking biographically) they are not where the poetry *begins*. They are part of the furniture, and in truth there is an abundance of such furniture, considering the room available. That is why there is such a clutter in the early poems. For where Lowell *begins* as a poet is approximately where Allen Tate had arrived by the time of *The Winter Sea*: with the sense of the loss and perhaps even the new irrelevance of the traditional religious-humanistic view of man and culture. I believe that the most intelligent critical statement I have read on this subject, or at least the one that is most relevant to the point of view I am developing, is one made in passing by Thomas Parkinson: "Behind the grander modern authors, who are now our classics, was a nineteenth century knowledge, and it was knowledge felt along the bone, of design that transcended the human. Lowell's mentor Allen Tate still participated in that knowledge, and it was the reason for his otherwise incomprehensible railing against solipsism." Parkinson then speaks of the loss of this sense of order, and some of its implications for art: "The principle of prior order [i.e., the 'design that transcended the human' of which he speaks above] means that the medium of art is not its essence but an inescapable material, and the art of the past twenty years represents first a surrender before media and second a surrender before a man-made order." Parkinson then remarks that "the abortive Catholicism of both Lowell and Tate was an effort toward evading or solving or protecting themselves against this very problem."[8]

Mr. Parkinson's conclusions are not precisely my own, since I am not sure, among other things, of the significance of anyone's "abortive Catholicism." But I certainly agree with the implications of most of Parkinson's remarks. The implications are particularly clear in the case of Lowell's early poems and the manner in which we must understand them. Those poems have for their principal motivating force the acute, simultaneous senses of enervation and desperation, violent reachings-out beyond the ego and lassitudinal retreats into the depths of the personality, where the spectres of privacy and ennui reign. The enormous energies of *Lord Weary's Castle* are sometimes suc-

8. *Robert Lowell: A Collection of Critical Essays*, pp. 148–49.

cessfully managed, more often they are not; but they are always deployments around the hollow center that is this sense of vacancy at the center of twentieth-century experience.

Let me put the matter in a different fashion. Robert Lowell's early work is in many ways a *rhetorical* poetry, and this rhetorical quality is a very odd thing in the twentieth century. It might be better to say that it is a poetry trying hard to be rhetorical, often in the grand manner, in the face of the fear that *any* rhetoric has ceased to be viable. It is neither accidental nor the result of simple perversity that rhetoric as an academic subject has vanished from our curriculum, replaced only by the vague feeling that *something* ought to be taught the young and by an amorphous subject matter that is called something different every year. Rhetoric presumes that there are people to talk to and principles that govern the manner in which we talk—principles that have something to do with the way the world is made. The idea of rhetoric is one that has nearly vanished from our discussions of and thinking about poetry. Perhaps the only major literary critic of the twentieth century to attempt to resurrect something close to the classical rhetorical theory of poetry is Yvor Winters, for it was not only Winters' exceptional pugnacity that distinguished him from his contemporaries. It is nearly literally true to say there was no one like him: Winters persisted in viewing poetry as a refinement of rhetoric.[9] As was so often the case, W. B. Yeats summarized the matter in an aphorism

9. This is, of course, an oversimplification, but it is not so ludicrous an oversimplification as most of the other things that have been said about Winters. Winters' extraordinary sensitivity toward, and fear of, the irrational; the sensuality of his own poetry (it *is* sensual poetry, in spite of those who persist in

that was both retrospective and prophetic. Unwilling, with Verlaine, to simply "wring the neck of rhetoric," Yeats's dictum that "we make out of the quarrel with others, rhetoric, but of the quarrel with ourselves, poetry" is nevertheless nearly definitive. Of the modern poet it is true that "like a long-legged fly upon the stream / His mind moves upon silence." It may be said that modern poets—meaning poets of the last 150 years or so—have substituted first the dramatic-ironic and then the meditative-reflexive modes for the classical rhetorical mode; it may even more confidently be said that the ghost of rhetoric has survived to haunt modern poetry.

It is precisely at this point that Allen Tate becomes so very relevant. I am arguing that he is not only relevant to an understanding of Lowell's abortive rhetoric, but that he is in a very particular way crucial for an understanding of the modern poetic mind (a necessary abstraction, even if it is a high-sounding and rather empty corporate lump). I am not arguing influence or even what is usually called importance; I am arguing centrality. Whether or not one "likes" Tate's poetry is irrelevant to this question, as is the reaction to Tate's claims to classicism or to the social views he seemed at one point to hold.

Let me put this as forcefully and even extravagantly as possible: there is no poetry so rhetoric-haunted as that of Tate. In a late essay, "A Southern Mode of the Imagination," Tate identifies that imagination as rhetorical. It always implies a listener, and the question is, how shall the listener be met and per-

dealing in cant phrases about "frigidity" and so on); and above all his frequent suggestion that poetry is a "technique of contemplation": these and other matters bring Winters, too, for all his classicism, into the twentieth century.

suaded? Whether that is true of the "southern imagination" I cannot say, but it is emphatically true of the classical imagination that it is a rhetorical imagination. This is one of the reasons that the classical and particularly the Latin world was always so close to Tate's work (as it has continued, of course, to be to Lowell's in a somewhat different manner); but this Latin, rhetorical mind nearly always stands in a reproving, chastening position in Tate's work, as part of the lost, dreamed world no longer available, even to a Southerner. Quite simply, there is no other poet of the first half of our century, major or minor, whose work is more conscious than Tate's of the claims that poetry made on Matthew Arnold at that crucial point in Arnold's career with which I began this essay: shall poetry move out into the world and can it? or shall poetry be of the mind and the person, and in so being figure itself forth into a world? To be even more explicit: Tate's "Ode to the Confederate Dead" has been often anthologized but seldom understood. Some understanding of what it implies is not only useful for discussions of Robert Lowell's early poetry, but it in many ways deserves to be considered as the central poem of the American 1930's. It is *the* poem that evokes the rhetorical problem and the whole question of the relevance of rhetoric. The man standing by the graveyard instructs himself to "turn your eyes to the immoderate past" and, having done so, fails to see anything except the wind blowing in the dried leaves of autumn. He talks, he expands, in the grand rhetoric of the Ciceronian orator:

> Turn to the inscrutable infantry rising
> Demons out of the earth—they will not last. . . .
> What shall we say of the bones, unclean,
> Whose verdurous anonymity will grow?

But to whom is this addressed? Who is expected to answer? The answer of course is that the question is directed in good post-Kantian fashion to the back of the speaker's own forehead. The poem is remarkable in a number of ways, but the one I want to emphasize is that it is remarkable among the poems of its time for the manner in which it deliberately calls up the rhetorical ideals of the older European civilization and butts its head against them. The poem ends in a series of what are only too obviously *rhetorical* questions that serve, among other things, to remind us of just how empty we have made the term "rhetorical question":

> Shall we take the act
> To the grave? Shall we, more hopeful, set up the grave
> In the house? The ravenous grave?

For rhetoric is predicated upon speech leading to action, and in this poem action is indeed carried to the grave. Any victory achieved is certainly Pyrrhic, for the poem has quite deliberately brought into light the dilemma that Arnold had sought to banish by an effort of the will. It is hardly too much to say that in "The Love Song of J. Alfred Prufrock" Eliot gave definitive expression to the erotics of isolation, and that fifteen years later in the "Ode" Tate gave definitive expression to the rhetoric of isolation (presumably neither eroticism or rhetoric was meant to occur in isolation, or even *could* occur in isolation; autoeroticism is something quite different). It has occasionally been argued against Tate's poem that it is *too* grand, and that the rhetoric of which I have been speaking is too self-conscious. The poem *is* both grand and self-conscious, and these features are part of its meaning. They are very much part of the reason that I see the poem as a central poem, and there is no important

28

American poet and no major poem of the period that would not in one way or another be illuminated by juxtaposition with the "Ode."

Once more, I am not claiming that "Ode to the Confederate Dead" is the "best" poem of the period, though by any standards it is a remarkable one. No one has ever done it justice. Certainly I did not in my book on Tate,[10] nor have I done so now. Surely any serious reader of modern literature knows how inadequate are the suggestions one occasionally still finds that the "Ode" is a sort of ambitious piece of "local" writing, though he will also recognize that the Southernness of the poem has something to do with its meaning. But, assuming that I am correct in ascribing such a representative quality to Tate's work and this poem, very few have ever glimpsed the issues that really lie in the "Ode."

Tate himself suggested some of the implications of the poem in an almost equally remarkable piece of writing, "Narcissus as Narcissus." This essay might be described as an exercise in self-explication, but if this is true it is so in an unusual manner. For all of the analytical procedure of Tate's essay, it is about as discursive and explanatory as a Henry James preface, and it is bewildering to see editors of textbooks printing it as a series of notes to the poem. The essay—both confronting and side-stepping its object, a poem that carries out a similar process on a larger scale—has the

10. Frank Kermode, reviewing the book for *The Sewanee Review*, justly censured it for, among greater errors, side-stepping "Ode to the Confederate Dead." He was right; the poem was too much for me, though I perhaps did not realize to what extent it was so. Mr. Kermode's own remarks on the poem—admittedly made in the context of a short review—suggest that he himself did not see the poem quite so fully as the elusive ideal critic should.

effect of holding a mirror up to a mirror. The poem, Tate says, is about "solipsism . . . the failure of the human personality to function objectively in nature and society." One wonders how many of those readers who approached the essay only for help in grappling with the "Ode" ever saw the issues that lurked behind the elegant philosophical diction, or what one of those same readers learned from an essay that, he surely thought, should have been a model of new-critical explication, since the critic was so familiar with his subject.

For if Matthew Arnold knew what he was doing in striking "Empedocles on Etna" from his canon, and if what Arnold sought to keep out of his poetry by sheer will-power has become the overwhelming subject of modern literature, then in Tate's work—not only in the "Ode"—we have practically a paradigm of the situation. I am arguing that the situation is nearly identical in Robert Lowell's poetry, and is particularly plain in his early poetry.

If one takes nearly any poem by either of the two, he will likely discover a situation that would correspond reasonably well to this abstract description: The protagonist, acutely aware of the acute sensibility by which he is possessed and estranged from intercourse with nature or society, employs his isolation by denouncing the excesses and iniquities of the society from which he *must* be separated if he is to retain his own humanity; or he broods on the limits of his own mortality in a language permeated with moral and religious overtones that nearly always have as well a strongly ironic element; or he sits stunned before the forces of history and nature, from which he is isolated and which he has little means of understanding. Sometimes these situations are combined, and frequently they are peopled with represented persons or cast into the language of a speaking person.

Certainly the abstraction is broad and cartoon-like, as if Roderick Usher were being evoked. There is little in this deliberately abstract description that would distinguish Tate or Lowell from many modern poets: for instance, Poe, Hart Crane, or even Browning in a sombre mood. Beyond the fact that the description is quite germane to one portion of my argument—that we can reasonably use the work of Tate and Lowell for exemplary purposes in discussing modern literature—I would suggest that when we get into the language of actual poems by the two men we have to deal with something more than the familiar romantic archetype. Here is the realm of real kinship, and it can be represented only by quotation. I have deliberately chosen examples from both early and late works of each man.

Here is Lowell in a kind of kinesthetic fury as the year draws to its close:

> O Christ, the spiralling years
> Slither with child and manger to a ball
> Of ice; and what is man? We tear our rags
> To hang the Furies by their itching ears,
> And the green needles nail us to the wall.
> (Lowell, "Christmas in Black Rock")

And here is Tate meditating the same season a dozen years earlier:

> now at last
> The going years, caught in an accurate glow,
> Reverse like balls englished upon green baize—
> Let them return, let the round trumpets blow
> The ancient crackle of the Christ's deep gaze.
> Deafened and blind, with senses yet unfound,

Am I, untutored to the after-wit
Of knowledge, knowing a nightmare has no sound. . . .
    (Tate, "Sonnets at Christmas")

Or consider what happens when the self is confronted in the nightmarish guise of the *Döppelganger*. This confrontation with the alter ego has been obsessive with both men, to a degree that is unusual even in our self-conscious age. It is the dark side of *Life Studies*, so to speak; Tate's direct treatment of the situation extends back at least to 1931 and the two-part "Records: I. A Dream, II. A Vision." The first passage is from Lowell's "Severed Head," one of the most powerful poems in *For the Union Dead*:

Then
    a man came toward me with a manuscript,
    scratching in last revisions with a pen
    that left no markings on the page, yet dripped
    a red ink dribble on us, as he pressed
    the little strip of plastic tubing clipped
    to feed it from his heart. His hand caressed
    my hand a moment, settled like a toad,
    lay clammy, comfortable, helpless, and at rest,
    although his veins seemed pulsing to explode.
    His suit was brushed and pressed too savagely;
    one sleeve was shorter than his shirt, and showed
    a glassy cuff-link with a butterfly
    inside. Nothing about him seemed to match,
    and yet I saw the bouillon of his eye
    was the same color as his frayed mustache,
    too brown, too bushy, lifted from an age
    when people wore mustaches. On each lash,
    a tear had snowballed. Then he shook his page,
    tore it to pieces, and began to twist
    and trample on the mangle in his rage.
    "Sometimes I ask myself, if I exist,"
    he grumbled. . . .

And here is another confrontation with the alter ego, this time in Tate's tighter *terza rima*, taken from "The

32

Maimed Man," a section of the late autobiographical poem (Tate did not reprint the section in his collected *Poems*). Like Lowell's figure, the apparition in Tate's poem is both personal and collective:

> as I sauntered down our street,
> I saw a young man there, headless, whose hand
> Hung limp; it dangled at his hidden feet
> I could not see how, in the fading band
> Of low light; nor did I feel alarm
> But felt, under my eyelids, grains of sand. . .
> I thought what civil greeting I might say;
> And could I leave the astonished oath unsaid
> That stuck to my palate in a gagging lump?
> Who could have told if he were live or dead?
> Retreating sideways to a ragged clump
> Of buckberry bushes in the vacant lot,
> I looked more closely at the purple stump—
> At the heart, three buttons down below the clot,
> Then down to where, the rigid shanks depending,
> Blue grass instead of feet grew in the slot.
> "If you live here," I said to the unbending
> Citizen, "it will not seem to you
> Improper if I linger on, defending
> Myself from what I hate but ought to do
> To put us in a fast ungreening grave
> Together, lest you turn out to be true
> And I publicly lose face."

One could go on, quoting passages where the two poets sound first like, then quite unlike each other. It would prove nothing. The only "proof" in this context is to sense the crucial situation that dominates the poetry of both men, in their later as well as their earlier work. Sometimes it is in the background, sometimes in the foreground; it goes through many modulations, but it is always there: the person, isolated in the moment, feels the narrow dimensions of his mortality pressing in upon him; a sense, nearly of vertigo, comes over him. Here is the crucial portion of Lowell's

"Skunk Hour"; it forms what might be called the climax of *Life Studies*:

> My mind's not right.
>
> A car radio bleats,
> "Love, O careless Love. . . ." I hear
> my ill-spirit sob in each blood cell,
> as if my hand were at its throat. . . .
> I myself am hell;
> nobody's here—
>
> only skunks, that search
> in the moonlight for a bite to eat.

This is the bottom; this is the point from which all the gropings begin and from which the recoveries must be made. This is the condition that lies behind Lowell's more public and political poems, and it runs through his *Imitations*. And here is something like Tate's version of the same situation. I venture to say that in "The Wolves," published in 1931, the condition enters into Tate's poetry more nakedly than anywhere else in his work. "The Wolves" is perhaps not the "confessional poetry" of thirty years later; it is more "literary." But the two poetries are blood kin:

> There are wolves in the next room waiting
> With heads bent low, thrust out, breathing
> At nothing in the dark; between them and me
> A white door patched with light from the hall
> Where it seems never (so still is the house)
> A man has walked from the front door to the stair.
> It has all been forever. Beasts claw the floor.
> I have brooded on angels and archfiends
> But no man has ever sat where the next room's
> Crowded with wolves, and for the honor of man
> I affirm that never have I before.

IV

We dread Eden, and of all Christian concepts there is
none we understand so well as the *felix culpa* and the
"fortunate fall"; not, certainly, because we anticipate
the salvation to which these Christian paradoxes
point, but because by means of sin and the fall we
managed to escape the seductions of peace and bliss.
                    (Lionel Trilling, *Beyond Culture*)

For both our faith and our physics are fascinated by
the vast voids inside and outside everything that
exists, by empty fields of tension, and by the in-
determinate motion of particles senselessly speeding
around one another in order to hide from themselves
the nothingness at the core of all things.
                    (Erich Heller, *The Disinherited Mind*)

Azure day
makes my agonized blue window bleaker.
Crows maunder on the petrified fairway.
Absence! My heart grows tense
as though a harpoon were sparring for the kill.
(This is the house for the "mentally ill.")
                    (Robert Lowell, "Waking in the Blue")

I have been talking about *tension*. What makes
the poetry of Tate and Lowell so representative is in
one very important sense the extraordinary feeling of
pressure generated in their poetry. The atmosphere in
a typical modern work is either unbearably tense, or it
is building toward that tension; or it is deliberately
turning aside from such tension (Ezra Pound's Orien-
tal work); or it seeks some remembered, or desired and
unobtainable peace (Randall Jarrell's "Lost World,"
and the lovely children's books he did with Maurice

Sendak; the greenhouse world of Roethke's earlier poems). Tension and lassitude: the extremes of our experience. The poems of *Life Studies* oscillate between these poles, and by the time of *For the Union Dead* and *Near the Ocean* a mood that might be described as desperate enervation dominates most of the poems. Tension: with our incredible facility, we have made it, too, banal. The word has become a critical cliché; it inhabits the poetry handbooks.

"Tension" has, of course, been part of our general vocabulary for a long time, and during the course of the nineteenth century it gradually became one of the indispensable words. One wonders whether the Western habit of dialectical thinking merely gave the scientists who discovered the forces of energy some convenient metaphors—poles, high tension, etc.—or whether it made possible the process of scientific discovery itself.[11] In any case, both the word and the condition of tension are implied in all of the dualisms of the Western philosophical classics, from Plato's sensible world/intelligible world to Kant's phenomenal/noumenal. The word and the condition are present in the soul/body dichotomies found everywhere in the thought of the early Christian church: the dichotomies Christian theologians so often ascribe to

11. This may be extreme; but perhaps it isn't. The discovery of the logic of discovery is certainly one of the distinctive features of the modern Western mind. As we are constantly being reminded, the Eastern mind is far older than the Western. We are also told that the sharp dualities of the Western mind differ markedly from the Eastern, and I am inclined to think this feature, more than any other, is what accounts for the origins and development of Western scientific thought. Differentiation, distinction, discrimination: These may be ambiguous virtues, but they are built into the Western mind. For the electricity metaphor I am indebted to Owen Barfield's early book, *History in English Words*.

36

Greek or Gnostic sources rather than Jewish or Christian ones. They are present in the separated but analogically related spheres of the world of nature and the world of grace in medieval thought. I strongly suspect that the roots of the modern condition in which I am interested are found in Christian syncretism. When the Christian church grafted the doctrine of the image of God onto the Delphic Oracle's advice to "know thyself" (which, of course, it did, quite consciously and deliberately), and came up with the ambiguities of *nosce teipsum*, incredible possibilities were opened up. For if man bore in his being the *imago dei*, every movement toward *self* knowledge then became a possibility for the revelation of mysteries and depths that the ancient world could not have anticipated. To know oneself, one must know at the same time, in some measure, God, and the world he has made.[12] And as our self-knowledge increases, we not only know more of God and the divine economy, but inevitably we know more of our separateness and of sin. It is a grand and treacherous pattern, and we can understand equally well Dante's joy in celebrating it and Nietzsche's in smashing it (as we can perhaps understand the other side of the coin that occasionally shows through in both Dante and in Nietzsche).

The idea and the word have been around a long time, then, but I think it is useful to pause and remind ourselves how "tension" became such a standard part of recent critical vocabularies. It is, of course, a strenuous mutation of the romantic aesthetic of uni-

12. A definitive statement on this, as on so many other medieval questions, may be found in Etienne Gilson's Gifford Lectures of 1931–1932, *The Spirit of Medieval Philosophy* (London, 1936).

ty, one that is pressed into service when you are none too confident of achieving the goal and when you realize how difficult the task is. And it came into the modern critical vocabulary primarily through Tate's "Tension in Poetry," an essay that is just about as tricky as "Narcissus as Narcissus." When we read it, the essay seems technical and procedural, which is very uncharacteristic of Tate. It is one of the great jokes of modern literary study that on that occasion Tate so succeeded in domesticating the fundamental violence of his vision that the key term has now been well absorbed into the very bloodless machinery for producing and describing poems that Tate spent so many years attacking. "Where is the tension in this poem, class?"—a question just about as macabre, when one stops to think of it, as those pedagogical grotesqueries of which Lionel Trilling reminds us in "On the Teaching of Modern Literature":

> The minds that give me the A papers and the B papers and even the C+ papers, move through the terrors and mysteries of modern literature like so many Parsifals, asking no questions at the behest of wonder and fear. Or like so many seminarists who have been systematically instructed in the constitution of Hell and the ways to damnation. Or like so many *readers*, entertained by moral horror stories. I have asked them to look into the Abyss . . . and the Abyss has greeted them with the grave courtesy of all objects of serious study, saying: "Interesting, am I not? And *exciting*, if you consider how deep I am and what dread beasts lie at my bottom. Have it well in mind that a knowledge of me contributes materially to your being whole, or well-rounded, men."

It might be worth while to look for a moment at Tate's essay and to see how he brought "tension" down to manageable size. He carefully kept his key word neutral and special, and it is only in such things as the slightly hyperbolic verb in his description of the origin of his term ("derived from lopping the prefixes off the logical terms *ex*tension and *in*tension") that we are reminded that whereas the term may be a special metaphor for this occasion it is also a general one. It recalls for us both the drive toward unity in the romantic tradition and the increasing difficulty of the task as that tradition faced the twentieth century. "My instructors identify consciousness with conflict," Yeats wrote in *A Vision*. The purpose of that conflict: to "struggle towards harmony, towards Unity of Being." That is not only Yeats speaking from his esoteric tradition, but the deepest artistic and spiritual aspirations of the nineteenth century. When Allen Tate describes the means by which the modern poet, romantic or Symbolist, may seek such unity and achieve it in his poem, we are struck not only by the accuracy or the inaccuracy of his insight but by the very martial language:

> Strategy would here indicate the point on the intensive-extensive scale at which the poet deploys his resources of meaning. The metaphysical poet as a rationalist begins at or near the extensive or denoting end of the line; the romantic or Symbolist at the other, intensive end; and each by a straining feat of the imagination tries to push his meanings as far as he can towards the opposite end, so as to occupy the entire scale.

Like the "solipsism" that is the subject of the "Ode to the Confederate Dead," the nearly bland, nearly philosophical language does not at first reading reveal its implications. But the "tension" and the "solipsism" are parts of the same condition: working alone and in the depths of his person, the poet attempts to find by language the means of breaking out from the personality, his monad. Even the most cunning and forceful means that may be found in language may not be adequate; language itself may not be adequate; the claustrophobia gets more intense; there may in fact be nothing to break out into; but the struggle must be continued (if necessary, by other means; which is why we have Father Ong, Professor McLuhan, and all of the young electronic prophets singing their songs).

I am deliberately attributing to Tate's essay some tones and nuances of meaning that are several degrees too intense to be directly justified by the text. I do so in order to emphasize that an aesthetic of "tension" is the appropriate language to use in describing a poetry *in extremis*, and the poetry of Tate is at least that, whatever else it may be. It is a poetry that has come just about as far as it can down this particular road.

And as I have said, this is where Lowell's poetry begins. "This is the end of the whale road and the whale," he wrote in "The Quaker Graveyard in Nantucket." It was the end of more than even that. Lowell's poetry begins at the end of an era, where poetry has moved nearly as far into the person as it can go, and the work of Wallace Stevens is there to demonstrate it; where poetry has tried the last resources of formal cunning to move outward into a larger sphere, and the work of T. S. Eliot is there to demonstrate it; and where poetry has also washed its hands of the whole narcissistic mess and resolved to get back into the world of men and things, and the work of William Carlos Williams is there to demonstrate *that*. Even deliberately limiting the examples to American poetry (and in spite of the opinion of Robert Bly and certain of his friends), it is hardly too much to say that all the alternatives had been tried. As Randall Jarrell said in 1942, it was "the end of the line." He was speaking of the end of "modernism," the remarkable period style in the arts that had prevailed since the second decade of the century; but more than that seemed to be drawing to a close.

Can we doubt that it is in at least some measure so? One tries to avoid a shoddy historical provincialism, the silly pride we take in feeling our days to be worse than others were. What answer can there be to the question: so when were things good? Nevertheless, as I look around, what my grandparents and parents would have called the signs of the times are plain (they took their apocalypses straight, in honest fundamentalist fashion, and had no traffic with literary oratory or discussions of archetypal images; we all have our versions of the easier past, and this is mine): new poetries that attempt to deny the destructive paradoxes of Western thought; the wild laughter of our novelists; the young, assuredly "in one another's arms" but, far from commending "whatever is begotten, born, and dies," instead singing that the times they are changing and proclaiming themselves the children of the future.

It is often said lately that in poetry such as that of Stevens, or Williams, or Charles Olson, or Robert Duncan, or someone else, we see a new poetry emerging that not only owes its existence to the emergence of a post-Christian world, but is predicated on an emphatic denial of the philosophical traditions that have dominated the Western mind since the Renaissance. This may yet prove true. I hope that at least we have gotten to the point where we can see

41

the destructive capacities inherent in those traditions with their impossible dichotomies (the quite artificial realms of "subject" and "object," the worlds of "value" and "fact," and so on), and where we can understand that a mode of thought that sharply separates the "I" not only from the material world but from all possible other "I's" makes the loneliness and frustration permeating modern art and culture quite inevitable. But at this point I cannot agree that a "new" vision of reality or a really "new" poetry has emerged. Such talk seems to me mostly wishful and often shallow thinking. To be sure, a poet like James Dickey, for instance, seems capable of transforming himself into a landscape with remarkable ease; and any number of young singers are able to merge with a grain of sand with an alacrity that can alarm those who daily grow less resilient. But I can neither believe that a "new vision" has emerged, nor can I admit the *inherent* inadequacy of the older visions. As our young people are saying, the trouble with American democracy is not that it is democracy, but that it has dismally failed to reach its ideals. One of Chesterton's witticisms that carries some weight is his remark that Christianity could hardly be called irrelevant when it hadn't been tried yet. I must return to these possibilities later. But Yeats's rough beast is still slouching toward Bethlehem, and if the cycle is in any sense ending, then the enormous relevance of the work of Tate and Lowell is at least partly in the fact that the turmoil accompanying the end of the cycle has gotten into their poetry in a special way.

V

AT the present moment it is Lowell, particularly, who is relevant. One of the more remarkable and praiseworthy qualities of Lowell as a poet and as a person is that he is so immediately involved in the scene we recognize as the life we live now. His poetry is topical; it is inhabited by people we know (we even know Lowell's Romans). As a person, he seems to be constantly showing up where the action is: with Eugene McCarthy, discussing, one presumes, not only poetry but the state of a society in which public language is automatically suspect, and with Norman Mailer, sharing the platform. One has to remind oneself occasionally that he is probably the most discussed poet of his generation. It is awkward to be discussing Lowell even more, and one should certainly desist if it were not that Lowell and his characters may be seen to be representative and symbolic, almost in the manner in which he himself has viewed Hawthorne and Melville. I also feel in a rather odd position vis-à-vis most of what has been written about Lowell. He has been praised and condemned, but I think too much of the criticism has dwelt on the highly discussable surface. It is just too easy to discuss the "case" of a New England patrician angered with his past and turned Catholic, who then departed the Catholic communion, who was jailed as a conscientious objector, who turned his own mental difficulties into the stuff of his poems. And if it is not precisely easy, it is at least obvious to search for the sources of his Christian imagery, to note his movement into a post-Christian mentality, to discuss the dangers of imitating European poets, or to debate the implications of confession and self-revelation in poetry. These are not bad things to do. There is certainly enough excuse for these kinds of criticism, for Lowell's is by no means an easy poetry. It often demands explication, and added to this there is the boldness of his various public stances, which have often attracted a great deal of comment. One of the frustrating but significant things about Lowell is that he often invites us to think about his poetry in ways that so easily slip into gossip.

All of these pursuits can so easily prevent us from asking what seem to me the really significant questions that we ought at this time to be asking about Lowell's poetry. One of the questions might be: what is there in his very great talent that it must be so self-destructive, so often determined to drive out the reasons for its own existence? Another question, closely related but larger, is: what is the fundamental pattern of experience in his poetry? I have been suggesting my answers to such questions by relating Tate and Lowell and by arguing that in their work we find a "pattern of experience" that is representative and typically modern. Before I can look at the pattern more closely in Lowell, I think that I ought to glance at several objections that might reasonably be raised against my arguments.

One objection is obvious: is it not beating the dead horse a little vigorously to direct attention to a typically "modern" pattern of experience, to call Lowell a "modern" poet? What else *could* he be? To this my response is that there have been a large number of intelligent and sophisticated men who have written about Lowell in a manner that implies that his poetry is to be explained only by his own "situation" and by a patchwork aesthetic derived from an odd assortment of past authors. Another objection is a little more complicated, and it is related to what seems to me to be the way Lowell is usually read by his critics. It might go like this: if Lowell is "modern," then he began as modern in the way you yourself indicate—in a manner reminiscent of Allen Tate and the more moribund features of the modern tradition as represented by Eliot. A good case might be made against me to the following effect. First, Tate and to a lesser extent Eliot, represent a compromised tradition, one that sees the poem as a formal occasion for the enclosure of experience—often violent experience—in language; this tradition has had a profoundly inhibiting effect on Lowell. Second, it was precisely his involvement with that sort of "modernity" represented by Tate, with all its elaborate, tattered rhetoric predicated upon a wornout world view, that Lowell had to overcome before he could emerge as a really authentic contemporary poet. No one has given more than a cursory glance at the relationship between Tate and Lowell of which I have spoken, but if they had, it would likely have been to say: Tate represented the kind of tradition-bound rhetoric, tightened like the head of a drum vibrating over emptiness, that Lowell had to slough off.

I cannot deny a certain *prima facie* plausibility to such views. If they were not plausible they would not be so commonly held. For my part, I think that the emphasis in such views is radically misplaced, and the inevitable result is what seems to me to be distortion and at times even obtuseness. Certainly I would not deny that Lowell's poetry has changed during the past twenty years, and the change at the time of *Life Studies* was particularly apparent and dramatic. The meaning of the developments in Lowell's style has been much debated, but the fact that such changes occurred is not in itself surprising, and an observer in the late 1940's might have picked up some clues to the impending changes from certain passages in *Lord Weary's Castle* that differ quite markedly from the tone of the rest of the book: for example, portions of "Between the Porch and the Altar," "Buttercups," "The First Sunday in Lent," "Mary Winslow," "In the Cage," and even the Edwards poems. It was clearly a case of his verse *having* to change if Lowell was to continue writing. In his early poetry he was plainly using certain tools nearly to their limits; they could be taken no further. But this is quite different from saying that Lowell was throwing off a tradition that was inhibiting him, or that he struck out on radically different tacks. Many critics see the changes in tone that began to occur in Lowell's poetry in the 1950's as a profound turning in his career; they see the emergence of an overtly quieter, more relaxed line as the symptom of something like a conversion in reverse. I think they are mistaken. The same critics usually go on to point out that the imagery of Lowell's poems grows increasingly secular (witness the earlier and later versions of "The Mills of the Kavanaughs"). They often point to a poem like "Beyond the Alps," frequently seeing it as Lowell turning his back on his earlier Catholicism (which it may be, but this is far too simple an "explanation" of that complex poem). Everyone agrees that about this time the poet's own person enters more directly into his poetry than it had before. But when these matters are taken to signify, as they usually are, that Lowell was finally chucking his false beginnings and getting serious, my response is, I not only believe that such criticism is mistaken but that it fails to perceive more important matters.

Once more I must refer to Lowell's remarkable friend and contemporary, Randall Jarrell. In his early review of *Lord Weary's Castle*, Jarrell discerned a fundamental pattern under all the theological trappings. It is not quite the same as the pattern with which I am concerned (and frankly I had forgotten Jarrell's essay as I wrote my own argument), but it is similar. Jarrell drew attention to a constant struggle in the poems between "necessity" and a drive towards "liberation." As was so often the case, Jarrell was far more relevant than many later critics; insights like this are worth far more than all the worrying about the exact nuances of Lowell's ecclesiastical symbolism, or the later wondering whether Lowell wasn't really better off without that symbolism. Jarrell wrote:

> The poems understand the world as a sort of conflict of opposites. In this struggle one opposite is that cake of custom in which all of us lie embedded like lungfish—the stasis or inertia of the stubborn self, the obstinate persistence in evil that is damnation. Into this realm of necessity the poems push everything that is closed, turned inward, incestuous, that blinds or binds. . . . But struggling within this like leaven, falling to it like light, is everything that is free or open, that grows or is willing to change: here is the generosity or openness or willingness that is itself salvation; here is "accessibility to experience"; this is the realm of freedom, of the Grace that has replaced the Law, of the perfect liberator whom the poet calls Christ.[13]

13. "From the Kingdom of Necessity," *Poetry and the Age* (New York, 1953), 188–89. This essay has also been reprinted in the Twentieth Century Views volume edited by Thomas Parkinson.

Jarrell's essay is still one of the best things ever written on Lowell, and not alone on his early poetry. With very little adjustment, it is relevant to Lowell's later work as well. For Lowell's poetry is very much of a piece. His late poetry is not separated sharply from his early poetry, but is a direct development from it. My major premise is that the fundamental situation, the relationship of the self and the world, has remained essentially the same throughout Lowell's poetry. That relationship has grown more intense, and though the images and situations have changed, the pattern has remained the same. The self—in the guise of various protagonists including one named "Robert Lowell"—confronts the world, the circumstances it has itself created and that press in; there is a direct or implied effort to understand and to break loose; a moment of stasis occurs as the effort fails (it may be the long stasis called "life," and one can even write sequences of poems about it); the self turns back in bitterness and irony. Occasionally—very rarely—there is a moment of freedom or affirmation, a hint that one can break through the frustration. This movement is as much in *Near the Ocean* as it is in *Lord Weary's Castle*, but the poet has been at it longer, and the strain is beginning to tell. Lowell may not be writing "Catholic" poetry any more (and it is silly to either praise or blame him for that; few of us seem to be doing much good on the religious question, and those who stand around and say that after all aren't we beyond religion and all that foolishness don't really help); his imagination is as apocalyptic as it ever was.

Furthermore, it remains a poetry haunted by the ideals and difficulties of rhetoric, by the possibilities of communication, of *talking to someone else*. In an interview, Lowell once referred humorously to the "goliath's armor of brazen metric" of his own earlier work. Metric is, among other things, a companion of rhetoric. It implies a contractual relation with someone other than yourself. When you give up the hope in any such relationship, metric begins to waver. You start looking for substitutes, saying that there must be more direct ways of handling the matter; you develop more "personal" metrics, variable feet, breath stresses that tally with the rhythm of the organism, and so on. After this goes on for a time, you begin to get either enervation, or reaction, or parody. As Lowell's poetry moves into and beyond *Life Studies*, the metric becomes muted and the rhetoric introverted. But the rhetorical process itself continues: in a later interview Lowell spoke of the difficulty of persuading the reader of *Life Studies* that he was encountering the "real" Robert Lowell. The self is still struggling to persuade—whom? of what? It remains a poetry predicated on struggle, violence: on tension. It attempts to break out into openness, and constantly asks, is this possible? The cry that breaks out of *Near the Ocean*

> O to break loose, like the chinook
> salmon jumping and falling back,
> nosing up to the impossible
> stone and bone-crushing waterfall

might well, in my view, be taken as a later response to the doomed protagonist of "The Slough of Despond," from *Lord Weary's Castle*:

> I walk upon the flood:
> My way is wayward; there is no way out:
> Now how the weary waters swell,—
> The tree is down in blood!
> All the bats of Babel flap about
> The rising sun of hell.

I do not want to seem to be in the position of minimizing the development in Lowell. His poetry has changed. I certainly don't believe that there is some kernel to be extracted from the poetry that makes any development irrelevant. The language of his poetry *has* changed, and as we all know, in poetry language is everything. Nor do I want to seem to be quarreling with those critics who prefer Lowell's later poetry to his earlier (a few would reverse the preference). What I do want to say is that it is silly to "refute" the earlier poetry by the later, and that the later develops directly out of the earlier.

VI

I don't know any way that I or anyone else could demonstrate that any writer does, or does not, give a peculiar sense of what it means to be living at the present moment. For after all, if someone else wishes to say that he happens to get more of that sense from Malcolm Lowry, or Samuel Beckett, or LeRoi Jones, or even from Studs Terkel's *Division Street: America*, what response can the critic make? He had better hope that writing itself has not recently been declared finally irrelevant. I have claimed that in Tate and Lowell we have something like a paradigm of the sense of the person being driven back in upon himself, and that this is a typical pattern of experience in modern poetry. I have said that this fundamental pattern of experience is something with which Lowell begins as a poet, that like Tate, he was brought to it by a certain tradition, that the pattern prevails throughout his career, and that there are no sharp breaks in that career. If what I have been saying is in any measure true, this pattern ought to be discernible in poetry from both his earlier and later periods. Therefore, I want to center most of the discussion that follows around several of his most important poems, with a few side excursions into other poems.

I want to begin with "The Quaker Graveyard in Nantucket," and to a certain extent the later discussion will be structured on the discussion of this poem. If Lowell's work as a whole has been much discussed, this poem in particular has been pored over more times than one can readily count. In fact, part of the reason I want to use the poem is that it *is* so well known. Then, too, I feel that "The Quaker Graveyard in Nantucket" is probably the best and most ambitious example of his early style. This isn't a particularly startling or unusual opinion, though some people would certainly question it.

"The Quaker Graveyard in Nantucket" should offer an interesting test case. Certainly Lowell's later poetry is about as unlike this as it can be, and he is no longer the promising, angry, young Catholic writer he was then. I hope to be able to show, however, that later poems like "Skunk Hour," "For the Union Dead," or "Waking Early Sunday Morning" are not so *completely* unlike the earlier work; indeed, that underneath their differences they all manifest, though certainly in different ways, what is essentially that pattern of experience of which I have been speaking.

I suppose that it is almost too obvious to say that "The Quaker Graveyard in Nantucket" is a kind of epitome of Lowell's early verse. The extremely dense rhetoric of the poem displays almost too fully the energy of his early work. I again use the word "rhetoric" deliberately; this is not only poetry in the high rhetorical manner, festooned with tropes and crammed with devices, but it is poetry flung into the face of a recalcitrant, unresponsive world. That opposing force which is the presupposition of any rhetoric is very much in evidence in the poem. The environment in "The Quaker Graveyard in Nantucket" is extraordinarily menacing. It is represented largely by the sea, a constant image in Lowell's work, which presses in upon the personality to such a degree that personality itself is nearly extinguished (I shall say more on these points later), and it is no exaggeration to say that the violence of the language is an attempt to wrestle some mode of salvation within reach. Here of course that mode of salvation is overtly the classical Christian mode, but the poem by no means asserts the Christian mode of salvation as an accomplished fact.

Probably the most constant preoccupation of Lowell's poetry has been with the question of salvation. I trust the use of the word "salvation" does not stamp me as having a hopelessly parochial mind, but "salvation" is one way of describing an essential feature of the pattern of experience with which I have been concerned. Another way is to speak more neutrally of the self's attempt to achieve authenticity (and I find *that* vocabulary uncomfortable), or to break through to freedom. Be that as it may, even Lowell's early poems with their Christian frame of reference constantly raise the possibility that *any* mode of salvation has disappeared from the world. The possibility that there is no salvation, no way out, becomes stronger in Lowell's later work. It would be quite wrong, however, to say that the question of salvation ever becomes irrelevant.

I have called the rhetoric of "The Quaker Grave-yard in Nantucket" dense, and that is one of the milder things that can be said of it. We are forcibly impressed with the feeling that this poetry is trying to hammer its way out of not only a personality but a literary crisis and trying to reach out for something new. The resemblance between Lowell's language in this poem and the history-obsessed rhetoric of Allen Tate's poems is very clear (Lowell once said that in portions of the poem he was trying to write like Tate, but it would never come quite right). It would hardly even be stretching the point too far to say that the poem is a kind of anthology of some of the chief effects and aspirations of poetry *d'entre deux guerres.*

Consider the diction. It almost desperately strives for physicality and particularity, and the struggle simultaneously reminds us of the mind's difficult access to the world. It is a noun-ridden poetry, and nearly every noun carries with it its definite article and a freight of adjectives. The verbs are mainly active, even wrenchingly so, and most of the modifiers might be called insistent ("screeching," "heaving," "coiling," and so on). Assonance and alliteration are very prominent, and occasionally they tumble so profusely through the lines as to threaten to turn the poem into a kinesthetic jag. The metrical and rhythmical elements are similarly suggestive. We realize at all times that we are in the presence of an immensely *knowing* poet, whose awareness seems to extend almost too far into every movement of his lines. We recognize the relevance of "Lycidas" to this poem almost immediately, and that precedent not only declares Lowell's intention of moving in the highest company, but on a more modest plane it gives us some perspective on his use of what is basically a pentameter line varied with trimeters, and the free use of rhyme. In about a third of the lines a caesura fights with the rhythm, often stopping the line in the last foot, and in nearly every line there's a struggle going on between the "iambic norm" and what is actually happening to the accents in the line. We have here constantly held before us the *difficulty* of poetry. And then there is one of Lowell's favorite devices, a way of using monosyllabic rhyme that is particularly apparent in this poem; it reminds us not only of the strenuousness of *this* poetry, but how strenuous poetry has become. The rhyme word has often the force of a smothered shock, which disturbs the sound and import of the language, but allows the syntax to go on relatively unimpeded, pretending that an order of things continues to reign. Like this:

> In the great ash-pit of Jehoshaphat
> The bones cry for the blood of the white whale,
> The fat flukes arch and whack about its ears,
> The death-lance churns into the sanctuary, tears
> The gun-blue swingle, heaving like a flail,
> And hacks the coiling life out: it works and drags
> And rips the sperm-whale's midriff into rags . . .

We know this is a "modern" poem in many ways, and not least by its persistent allusiveness to a very wide range of earlier literature; Milton, Melville, Thoreau, and the Old Testament are probably the chief contributors. And through the whole runs mingled ecclesiastical and sexual symbolism, attempting to join the depths and the hoped-for heights of life. The total effect of all this is not very pretty, but it is awfully arresting. It is such a display that it inevitably makes one wonder what the poet was trying to prove. Certainly it was nothing so simple as virtuosity.

In its courting of the rhetorical mode, "The Quaker Graveyard in Nantucket" deserves to be compared with Tate's "Ode to the Confederate Dead."[14] Certainly the poem is not so conscious of as wide a range of implications as Tate's, but like the earlier work it *does* raise the questions of the relevance and meaning of rhetoric. And it is one generation further into the questions. I hope it is not a cheap paradox to say that the rhetoric of Lowell's poem seems to conceal the collapse of rhetoric. There is a strange emptiness behind all the mounting of the grand style. Rhetoric is predicated upon people talking and others listening, and in "The Quaker Graveyard in Nantucket" there is a peculiar absence of personality. This gives a very odd effect, particularly when it is combined with the immense deployment of poetic resources in the poem, for there are very few twentieth-century poems more impersonal (not in Eliot's sense) than "The Quaker Graveyard in Nantucket." In retrospect, the impersonality seems most unusual, for Lowell was soon to write not only the dramatic (if often awkward) poems of *The Mills of the Kavanaughs*, but —after the break from 1951 to 1959 in his publication career—a poetry so very personal that it was shortly being labelled "confessional." We cannot explain the fact simply by saying that this poem is an early work. Much of *Lord Weary's Castle* is extremely personal in ways that "The Quaker Graveyard in Nantucket" is not.

It may seem that these observations have placed my own theory in jeopardy: that in Lowell one sees

14. In another sense "For the Union Dead" deserves the comparison. It is an even later poem than "The Quaker Graveyard in Nantucket." And I am not being in the least facetious when I observe that, between their two titles and their two poems, the poets have fairly covered the field.

the fundamental pattern in which the threatened self attempts to deal with the environment, to at least stand before nature, and if it cannot mold it then to at least find an equilibrium in or beyond nature. I do not really think the thesis is in jeopardy, however. On the contrary, I think that the poem makes it even stronger.

It is true that in this poem there is no point at which a human personality seems to appear directly. Certainly there is no identifiable "voice," even though there is seemingly someone talking, speaking of the "we" who discover the corpse in the first section; the poem speaks of "my cousin," and therefore it presumably refers to Lowell's own experience; but the voice seems to emanate from no specific point. There is no placing of a person at a point in a landscape as there is in so much of Lowell's other poetry—"Christmas in Black Rock," to choose just one of many examples from *Lord Weary's Castle*. I say this in spite of the use to which the poem puts Nantucket, a very definite place, and its insistent references to Madaket, Cape Cod, 'Sconset, Wood's Hole, Martha's Vineyard. As we read the poem we know we are dealing with the work of a New Englander, and that not only some geographical references but what is called "the New England Mind" are deeply involved here. But in spite of this there is really no definition of the landscape; it is a landscape overwhelmed by history. The poem is all environment, and the environment is the limitless sea.

The absence of either substantial persons or a locatable voice in the poem is partly due to the generalizing effect of the grand style, and we certainly recognize that the poet has chosen deliberately to avoid the dramatic procedures of his other poems in order to give impersonality and authority to a poem that almost aggressively demands that we compare it with the great elegies of the English tradition. I think there is another factor at work here that is more important, and to do it justice we have to look at the context of "The Quaker Graveyard." It is not only a single poem, it is part of a book, and in *Lord Weary's Castle* it seems to me significant that the personality has proceeded through the alternately ecstatic and harrowing experience of "Exile's Return," "The Holy Innocents," "Colloquy in Black Rock," "Christmas in Black Rock," and "New Year's Day." In only one of these poems, "Colloquy in Black Rock," is the first person prominently used, but they are all far more clear in their placement of the voice than is "The Quaker Graveyard." After "The Quaker Graveyard" the self emerges, chastened and besieged, in "The First Sunday in Lent" and the other later poems in the book (including the dramatized personae of the Edwards poems).

What personality does get into "The Quaker Graveyard" fares very badly, far worse than Matthew Arnold could have predicted. There is a great deal of action in the poem, but it is all happening *to* the self; it is limp before the onslaught of the sea, which is both implacable nature triumphing over human desire and history running out of control. There are several guises in which human personality is represented in the poem. There is Warren Winslow, who has vanished into the sea more thoroughly than Edward King ever vanished into the pastoral landscape of "Lycidas": the defeated self—"All you recovered from Poseidon died / With you, my cousin." The poem repeatedly evokes the over-reaching self in the person of Melville's Ahab, whom Lowell sees as one of the crucial avatars of the American character. And there are the avaricious Quaker sailors, breaking their backs against history. All of these—Winslow, Ahab, the Quakers—have in one form or another challenged the sea, and it has triumphed. The implication is clear that defeat awaits all sailors ("Atlantic, you are fouled with the blue sailors"), and all men are sailors.

We know that a man named Robert Lowell wrote the poem, and that it is "about" his cousin. But this is the subject of the poem to about the same extent that Confederate soldiers were the subject of Tate's "Ode." It is as if, lying behind the entire complicated fabric of the poem, a general human consciousness were seeking to engage the world rather than to merely suffer it, looking for room to stand. But nowhere in the poem does it really succeed, and it is nearly as if the poet had decided not to risk letting any individuals directly into this arena, where they could so obviously not survive at all: there are only the unnamed sailors, the corpse, and the tissue of historical allusions. There is a striking lack of first person pronouns, and those that are present are submerged; the only real agent in the poem is the sea.

I am not urging these things as facts "against" the poem, for this is certainly one of Lowell's most memorable early works. But as I remarked in connection with Tate's "Ode," its victories are distinctly Pyrrhic. Perhaps, at least to a certain type of poet, these are the only ones available. There can be no doubt that the very absence of human potency is one of the poem's chief meanings. This failure of energy, the inability of the personality to deal fruitfully with the world, is really the most crucial element in the pattern of experience that I have been describing, and in fact Lowell's attention has tended to become fixed at this point. And it is not much of an exaggeration to say that there are few poems by Lowell in which the human personality is more at bay than in "The Quaker Graveyard in Nantucket." Not in the intensely personal poems of the penultimate section of *Life Studies*, nor in "The Severed Head," "Myopia: a Night," or the other poems of *For the Union Dead*, nor even in the profoundly desolate poems of *Near the Ocean*, is the person driven into a much tighter corner, even though in the later poems we may be able to observe the condition more closely. Lowell was much more a believer in the possibilities of rhetoric in his early work, and the rhetorical machinery of "The Quaker Graveyard" tends to conceal from us just how close the earlier and later poetry in many ways are. This is why it makes very little sense to divide Lowell's career sharply into quite different "early" and "later" poetries. Nearly all of Lowell's critics prefer the more personal and less flashy later style, and on the whole I do not quarrel with the judgment, though I do not think the later style represents quite as clear a gain as many others seem to. I think, furthermore, that we should notice that while the later poetry is more open and direct, and that in it we get a far clearer experience of the poet speaking, the sense of the impotence of the person and the forces that repress him remain Lowell's major subject. There seem to me to have been no really major shifts in his sensibility.

Lowell's capacity for moral indignation, one of the more attractive features of his work, has remained high. Poets and rhetoricians have always found plenty to denounce in their societies, but even considered in this long tradition, Lowell is unusual. In *Lord Weary's Castle* one encounters everywhere the rage the poet turns on New England, that in the name of piety removed wilderness, whales, Indians, and any other obstacle that blocked the path to Zion. In *Life Studies* the tone is more intimate, wryer; it is more frequently turned inward, and toward the family; but even in that volume we find:

> Our wheels no longer move.
> Look, the fixed stars, all just alike
> as lack-land atoms, split apart,
> and the Republic summons Ike,
> the mausoleum in her heart.

And the final image of *For the Union Dead* calls up echoes of "Concord," in *Lord Weary's Castle*, where "Ten thousand Fords are idle here in search / Of a Tradition":

> Everywhere,
> giant finned cars nose forward like fish;
> a savage servility
> slides by on grease.

In everything Lowell has written, from the early, powerfully stumbling poems in *Land of Unlikeness* to the very recent poetry, we hear what is essentially the same voice, commenting on the outrages of its society.

When you turn this capacity for moral outrage inside out, it becomes that estrangement of the personality from its environment which I have commented on and which is always seen in the implacability and impenetrability of nature in Lowell's poems. Consider for example the role of the sea in his work. It is one of Lowell's really obsessive images, and whereas in Allen Tate's poetry water retains at least the vestiges of its life-giving powers, in Lowell it is nearly always threatening. The Sea is the chief presence and actor of "The Quaker Graveyard in Nantucket," and while Matthew Arnold could stand on the cliffs listening to the withdrawal of the sea, in Lowell's poem it is whipped by winds, rushing out of its bloodied depths. The Quaker sailors go to their deaths crying, "If God himself had not been on our side, / When the Atlantic rose against us, why, / Then it had swallowed us up quick," but we are left to ponder God's enigmatic providence and to observe that no one who encounters this sea survives. In the later poems the situation is similar even though, as with everything else in Lowell, the later encounters with the sea are transacted on a much more personal basis. The first poem of *For the Union Dead* is called simply "Water." In it a man and a woman sit by the sea:

> The sea drenched the rock
> at our feet all day,
> and kept tearing away
> flake after flake.

This is certainly much *quieter* than "The Quaker Graveyard," and there are at least people here, but the water is still threatening:

> We wished our two souls
> might return like gulls
> to the rock. In the end,
> the water was too cold for us.

In *Near the Ocean*, as the title warns us, the encounter with the sea is constant. In the earlier poems there was a mounting tension as the self attempted to summon energy to meet the occasion; even in a poem like "Water" there is the desire, if a wistful one, for the personality to stand with some security. But by the time of *Near the Ocean*, though we get the reaffirmed wish of the self to break through, if not to tranquillity then at least to something like authentic experience, this is accomplished in the somewhat desperate image of the spawning salmon:

> O to break loose, like the chinook
> salmon jumping and falling back,
> nosing up to the impossible
> stone and bone-crushing waterfall—
> raw-jawed, weak-fleshed there, stopped by ten
> steps of the roaring ladder, and then
> to clear the top on the last try,
> alive enough to spawn and die.

The encounter with the water formerly provoked tension; now all dies into lassitude:

> Sleep, sleep. The ocean, grinding stones,
> can only speak the present tense;
> nothing will age, nothing will last,
> or take corruption from the past.

The line of development is a direct one. From *Lord Weary's Castle* right on through *Near the Ocean* the self butts its head against the body of fate—the evils of the world and the responding ills within—and seeks a way through. Lowell has frequently been brilliantly successful in objectifying the process; perhaps in *Life Studies* he succeeded in taking his poetry just about as far as it could go toward the point where the personality is driven back upon its last resources. But when that point is reached it becomes a question of how much further one can proceed along that line, and the answers to this question that are offered by his most recent poetry are bleak. In Lowell's earlier poems, up through *Life Studies* and on into at least some of *For the Union Dead* the internal struggle found ways of transmitting its energy into a correspondingly energetic poetry. The assumption underlying such an art, one that can be described by the aesthetics of tension, is that there is some possibility of maintaining the integrity of the person; the struggle is always conducted with the possibility of breaking through the wall of

circumstance, or at least with the dignity and importance of the struggle kept in view.

This assumption seems to be wearing very thin indeed in Lowell's latest work.[15] For this reason, though
his preoccupation with the pressures of mortality is as
great as ever, the pattern of experience that I have described has become severely attenuated, and one of the
most interesting movements in his poetry has nearly
vanished. This point occurs at the moment when a
kind of tentative tranquillity emerges from in the
midst of the violence. One version of this movement
has always occurred in Lowell's work at that point
where an occasional short poem—such as "Buttercups" in *Lord Weary's Castle* or "Father's Bedroom"
in *Life Studies*—seems to interrupt the progress of the
volume by its softer, almost memorializing, manner—
a movement back into memory, a spot-in-time that
seems free at least for the moment from self-lacera-
tion.

But I am more concerned with a subtler and more

15. One of the hazards of writing about a poet as pro-
lific as Lowell is that he may at any moment make one's observations dated by publishing another book. *Notebook of a Year:
1967–1968* (New York: Farrar, Straus & Giroux, Inc., 1969) ap-
peared after this essay was written. Consequently, when a
phrase like "Lowell's recent poetry" is used in this essay, it
cannot be taken to refer to anything published after *Near the
Ocean*. I have not had time to read Lowell's new book carefully, although what reading I have done reveals many poignant
passages and some of extraordinary brilliance. There are four
poems to Allen Tate in the book, including a very moving one
on the death of Tate's infant son.

I must say that *Notebook of a Year: 1967–1968* confirms
my feeling that in this essay I have invented a true but myth-
ological monster ("Pity the Monsters!"); a real monster whose
circumference is everywhere and center nowhere (to paraphrase
Coleridge); and called, for convenience, Robert Lowell.

interesting process that occurs in a number of his better poems where for a moment we get a glimpse of something lying beyond the tangle and frustration. It is never more than a glimpse; Lowell's poetry never holds out any real passage through the difficulties, for all its preoccupation with mortality and salvation. But occasionally—indeed so rarely that it is startling when it occurs—there is an image or passage that runs against the prevailing texture and stands in an almost rebuking fashion against the established current of the poem. Rare as these passages have been in Lowell's poetry, they have occurred often enough to remind us what the thresh and wrestle was all about. In spite of their completely different metaphorical bases and methods of procedure, three examples where the essentially similar process appears are in, once more, "The Quaker Graveyard in Nantucket," in "Skunk Hour" (the penultimate poem of *Life Studies* in the first paperback printing; the last poem of the volume in other printings), and in "Colonel Shaw and the Massachusetts' 54th" (which was the final poem of *Life Studies* in the first paperback edition, but later was retitled "For the Union Dead"; it stands out even more from the context of the volume for which it became the title poem than it did from *Life Studies*). I do not think the grouping of these three poems is as arbitrary as it might at first appear. I also think that it is more than mere sanguinity which makes me think it instructive to link the images of Our Lady of Walsingham, the mother skunk and her young, and the statuary of the Colonel and his bronze Negroes, and to observe the way these images function in their respective poems.

I have spoken enough of "The Quaker Graveyard

in Nantucket" to make clear the major qualities I see in that poem, and in the uncontrollable sea that dominates it. "Skunk Hour" is a far more personal, a much quieter, poem, but it shares with "The Quaker Graveyard in Nantucket" the sense of things running out of control, the mind unable to deal with the situation. If there is anything that the style of "Skunk Hour" is *not*, it is *grand*. Lowell does not take on the processes of history nor plunge into the watery depths quite so easily as he did earlier. Instead, "Skunk Hour" offers "Nautilus Island's hermit heiress," "our summer millionaire," "our fairy decorator"—less immediately impressive than the Quakers in the "mad scramble of their lives" in the earlier poem, but not so different after all, and certainly closer at hand. The cry of "my mind's not right" could never have been admitted into "The Quaker Graveyard in Nantucket"; it is too intimate, too personal (though it recalls some of the other poems of *Lord Weary's Castle*). And the climax of "Skunk Hour" is managed more cleanly and directly than anything in the earlier poem:

> I hear
> my ill-spirit sob in each blood cell,
> as if my hand were at its throat. . . .
> I myself am hell;
> nobody's here

The echo of Milton's Satan and the terse "nobody's here" remind us that if the style has changed, "Skunk Hour" remembers both the loftiness and the emptiness of the earlier poem.

"For the Union Dead" (to use its later title) is a poem poised somewhere between the intimacy of "Skunk Hour" and the immensity of "The Quaker Graveyard in Nantucket," and as the poet represents himself standing before a tank in the old South Boston Aquarium there is something of each of the other two poems present:

> Once my nose crawled like a snail on the glass;
> my hand tingled
> to burst the bubbles
> drifting from the noses of the cowed, compliant fish.

> My hand draws back. I often sigh still
> for the dark downward and vegetating kingdom
> of the fish and reptile.

This is neither as vast as "The Quaker Graveyard in Nantucket" nor as close as "Skunk Hour," but this poem nevertheless generates its own peculiar pressures that draw into themselves all of the overtones of the earlier poems, and more. The walled-off, separated images of "For the Union Dead" yearn sadly outward, only to come up against the walls that seal the personality into itself: the glass of the aquarium. And this bleakness within is matched by a bleakness without, the images of a society we recognize too well: the "commercial photograph [of] Hiroshima boiling," the "drained faces of Negro children," the "giant finned cars": "savage servility." I have already presumed to speak of "salvation" so I will not hesitate to use here another theological word: hell. The word comes naturally in discussing Lowell, and he himself used it at the climax of "Skunk Hour." It is not too much to say that in the three poems in question we have three views of hell. If one wanted to take account of the development of Lowell's style, the progress of his prevailing vocabulary and metaphors, one might say that the first view of hell is described in historical and theological language, the second in psychological language, the third in social and political language. But it really would not do, it is too neat and schematic.

Hell is hell, and its essence is isolation, separateness: consciousness hermetically sealed from life, life itself decaying; the passive observer, the disintegrated world. Here is a part of hell, as it appears in "For the Union Dead":

> Behind their cage
> yellow dinosaur steamshovels were grunting
> as they cropped up tons of mush and grass
> to gouge their underworld garage. . . .
>
> The Aquarium is gone. Everywhere,
> giant finned cars nose forward like fish;
> a savage servility
> slides by on grease.

Against these images of hell, in each of the three poems Lowell poses an image of order or stability. These images are scarcely bursting with affirmation, and in each the possibilities they represent exist most precariously. I assume that Lowell was speaking metaphorically when, in a very early review of Hopkins, he said that poetry always had union with God in view (and this is no place to ask the question of how literally a poet dare mean his metaphors, or whether Lowell's earlier or later metaphors are more valid). If "union with God" shall be read as a metaphor for freedom, fertility, openness—all those possibilities in man's experience that have made him desire and at times believe in immortality—then these three points are among those in Lowell's poetry at which he has come closest to it.

The image of Our Lady of Walsingham in "The Quaker Graveyard in Nantucket" is one of the quieter as well as one of the best known manifestations of Lowell's early Catholicism. The passage, adapted from E. I. Watkin's *Catholic Art and Culture*, has often been singled out as an example of a more devotional or even

mystical quality in Lowell's earlier work. It is also easy
to say that the passage is parochial, that it represents
the kind of inhibiting ties with an outworn tradition
from which he was fortunately able to free himself.
There is no doubt, reading from the perspective of
Life Studies, that such passages as "much against my
will / I left the city of God where it belongs" or "I
was a fire-breathing Catholic C. O." are ironic back-
ward glances by Lowell at his own past. But such con-
siderations leave untouched the points I am trying to
make. For one thing, there is the singular diffidence
with which this poem's "vision" is presented:

> As before,
> This face, for centuries a memory,
> *Non est species, neque decor,*
> Expressionless, expresses God: it goes
> Past castled Sion. She knows what God knows,
> Not Calvary's cross nor crib at Bethlehem
> Now, and the world shall come to Walsingham.

In spite of the clear presence of Watkin's language in
the passage, one could hardly say that what Lowell has
done with it presents a model of Christian orthodoxy.
Our Lady, knowing "what God knows," represents a
beckoning but unattainable tranquillity, leaving the
reader still with the problem of what it is that God
knows and what its relation may be to the world of
this poem. Furthermore, the passage is not very well
assimilated into the rest of the poem. I do not accept
those interpretations that would explain this lack of
assimilation as the result of poor workmanship, or
would suggest that the passage represents something
inessential and alien. It rather seems to me that the
passage, ambiguous and tentative though it may be,
is deliberately counter-balanced against the frenetic
activity of the other six sections, and for that matter

most of the rest of *Lord Weary's Castle*. There is no guarantee, and, indeed, little hope, that the world will in fact "come to Walsingham" or that the self can break through to freedom, but there is here at least an image of that possibility and it stands rebuking, if not healing, the violence that reigns at all other points.

The situation is similar in "Skunk Hour." I suppose that, depending on one's point of view, my comparison of the image of Our Lady to that of the skunks of the later poem could seem either ludicrous or sacrilegious. The distinctions between sacred and secular grow constantly dimmer, and even if we still make them they shouldn't hide the fact that the skunks in the later poem also stand in the midst of violence and represent a movement away from it toward sanity and repose. They are about as far "below" the human situation as Our Lady of Walsingham is "above" it, and their animal equilibrium as they cheerfully root through the garbage that repels higher, more fastidious but less stable, mentalities is probably equally unattainable:

> I myself am hell;
> nobody's here—
>
> only skunks, that search
> in the moonlight for a bite to eat.
> They march on their soles up Main Street:
> white stripes, moonstruck eyes' red fire
> under the chalk-dry and spar spire
> of the Trinitarian Church.
>
> I stand on top
> of our back steps and breathe the rich air—
> a mother skunk with her column of kittens swills
>   the garbage pail.
> She jabs her wedge-head in a cup
> of sour cream, drops her ostrich tail,
> and will not scare.

There they are. If what they represent is a kind of minimal courage and dignity, that much is nevertheless present.

In "For the Union Dead" the corresponding image of order, of liberty and dignity, is human, and so it seems closer to our daily affairs than either skunks or a destroyed shrine to the Virgin. And in a way this is true. But Colonel Shaw, who in some measure chose his fate and did not merely submit to it, is present in Boston only as a bronze statue. The monument to Colonel Shaw and his Negroes "sticks like a fishbone / in the City's throat." It stands over against a servile society, a Boston no prettier here than it was in *Lord Weary's Castle*. It is the city we know too well, the city we have created, and it could wear many other names beside Boston (though of course Lowell's poem requires Boston's special resonance). In this poem we watch something like a miniature version of the process by which we have accustomed ourselves to brutality:

> Shaw's father wanted no monument
> except the ditch,
> where his son's body was thrown
> and lost with his "niggers."
>
> The ditch is nearer.
> There are no statues for the last war here;
> on Boylston Street, a commercial photograph
> shows Hiroshima boiling
>
> over a Mosler Safe, the "Rock of Ages"
> that survived the blast. Space is nearer.
> When I crouch to my television set,
> the drained faces of Negro school-children
> rise like balloons.

Still, what the Colonel represents is real enough, even if the only way it can get into this scene is as a piece of statuary: action frozen, but nevertheless the possibility of action, and even of dignity:

> He is out of bounds now. He rejoices in man's lovely,
> peculiar power to choose life and die—
> when he leads his black soldiers to death,
> he cannot bend his back.

As I have said, such moments have always been rare in Lowell. Even in these examples it is only in "Skunk Hour" that the image of wholeness and sanity closes the poem; in the other two the poem moves back into the contrary vision of moil and decay. One hesitates to risk too great a judgment on the presence or absence of such a tentative pattern, and one would be naïve to count the "images of affirmation" or something similar in a poet's work and assign it its appropriate value accordingly. But there is much at issue; there is an entire attitude toward our experience involved here. It seems to me that poetry such as Lowell's, which constantly asks us to participate in profound crisis, must also rest much of its case on the possibility of a break into openness, or else what is the point? That there is no point? We rightly ask that such moments be *earned* by the poetry, but we also have a right to believe they are necessary to give truly substantial meaning to the poetry. The poet's talents may be great, his misery exemplary, but there inevitably comes the time at which, in spite of the talent, misery becomes redundant: we have troubles of our own. If we have no hope of at least momentarily seeing into the life of things or of finding a way to live with them, it is an imposition to ask us to attend to an art in which we are merely at the mercy of things.

This is in one sense overly harsh, and the critic has little right to lecture in such circumstances. Lowell is an extraordinary poet, and it is his privilege to impose on us a good deal. Nevertheless, it seems to me that the conditions revealed in his recent poetry are disquieting, and that the quality that disturbs one in Lowell's recent poetry is altogether different from that disturbance we receive in the work of a poet who has a quite different perspective from our own and challenges us to see as he does; or from the poet who denounces us for our blindness. It is the very lack of challenge, the denial of *any* vitality in Lowell's later work, that is disturbing. We no longer get either the energy of conflict or those tentative moments in which, in spite of the wretchedness, we are convinced that there is yet something in this human condition that has value. I dare not assert categorically that this is the case with Lowell's late poetry, but only that it seems so to me; and that it is possibly in the "Hawthorne" poem of *For the Union Dead* that we have the last place in Lowell's work where any sense of the real value of the struggle appears:

> Even this shy distrustful ego
> sometimes walked on top of the blazing roof. . . .
>
> His hard
> survivor's smile is touched with fire.
>
> Leave him alone for a moment or two,
> and you'll see him with his head
> bent down, brooding, brooding,
> eyes fixed on some chip,
> some stone, some common plant,
> the commonest thing,
> as if it were the clue.
> The disturbed eyes rise,
> furtive, foiled, dissatisfied
> from meditation on the true
> and insignificant.

In the rest of the book, with the exception of the title poem and possibly of "Jonathan Edwards in Western Massachusetts," and in all of *Near the Ocean*, there is the sense that the battle of the self has finally met circumstances too strong to be withstood. In poem after poem we contemplate the sad isolation of the self from nature; the pattern, the impulse toward action that formerly produced "tension" has become purely intransitive, reflexive. The self has ceased to attempt transcendence; nor does it attempt to transfigure and make radiant the immanent. It is caught in something like pure ennui, which was always the threatened terminus of this mode of perceiving experience. Lowell is still capable of the poem that wryly acknowledges the situation:

> Tenth Muse, Oh my heart-felt Sloth,
> how often now you come to my bed,
> thin as a canvas in your white and red
> check dresses like a table cloth,
> my Dearest, settling like my shroud! . . .

> But I suppose even God was born
> too late to trust the old religion—
> all those settings out
> that never left the ground,
> beginning in wisdom, dying in doubt.

But the prevailing tone is that of loneliness, a sense that there is nothing to be done:

> Young, my eyes began to fail.
> Nothing! No oil
> for the eye, nothing to pour
> on those waters or flames.
> I am tired. Everyone's tired of my turmoil.
> ("Eye and Tooth," *For the Union Dead*)

> We watch the logs fall. Fire once gone,
> we're done for: we escape the sun,

> rising and setting, a red coal,
> until it cinders like the soul.
> Great ash and sun of freedom, give
> us this day the warmth to live,
> and face the household fire. We turn
> our backs, and feel the whiskey burn.
> ("Fourth of July in Maine," *Near the Ocean*)

Only the memory of the possibility remains; this rhetoric has no confidence in itself, let alone any possible subject to which it might be addressed. The voice in this poetry is not only alone; it seems to have lost its tenderness, anger, irony; there is only nostalgia. Yet the nostalgia retains, or has potentially within it, a cutting edge, one honed on an awareness of greater possibilities. Here is a stanza from an earlier version of "Waking Early Sunday Morning" (from the *New York Review*, August 5, 1965). Lowell deleted it before the publication of *Near the Ocean*:

> Empty, irresolute, ashamed,
> when the sacred texts are named,
> I lie here on my bed apart,
> and when I look into my heart,
> I discover none of the great
> subjects: death, friendship, love and hate—
> only old china doorknobs, sad,
> slight, useless things to calm the mad.

I will not speculate on Lowell's motives for canceling the stanza; for one reason or another it dissatisfied him. But from one point of view, I wish he'd left it in, because such passages so clearly force us to ask the question: what are the alternatives remaining open to the modern artist or thinker? It is presumptuous for an essayist to raise such a question. How can it possibly be answered by anyone? Nevertheless, I suggest that the mode of facing experience that we have been considering in this essay makes it imperative that we think most carefully of such questions and at least attempt to find some answers. Let me merely suggest some alternatives.

The first and on the face of it the most improbable alternative is to attempt, as Arnold said, to find the "great subjects," to find a world where, as Lowell's stanza has it, it is not foolish or tedious to speak of death, friendship, love and hate *as* "great subjects." In other words, we would have to find some way to believe in the "sacred texts"; in less vivid language, to believe in a real principle of order in the world to which poetry and social action alike respond. As I say, this may seem improbable. William James aside, how does one will belief? We have received notice that God is dead, and we know that principles of order are difficult to come by. We can, of course, refuse to accept the notice of death, as Erich Heller has said[16] (although I personally believe that what many people have meant by "God" *is* dead, and a very good thing, too). In any case, this "alternative" is to find a principle of order that will lead us to something like a metaphysics; for we should be finding out by now that we are not making it very well on mere aesthetics. If this seems simplistic or innocent, we may look at other alternatives.

A second is to disbelieve in any principle of order other than that of the creative human intelligence. Historically it has not been true that these two alternatives have been mutually exclusive. The Judaeo-Christian tradition has seen man's intelligence as the reflection of divine creative activity: man created in

16. In "The Hazard of Modern Poetry," in *The Disinherited Mind* (Cleveland, 1959). Heller's work—particularly this essay and "Rilke and Nietzsche, with a Discourse on Thought, Belief and Poetry," as well as *The Artist's Journey into the Interior*—are very relevant.

the image of God. Coleridge insisted on both a primary and secondary imagination, and Kant after all *did* write his second and third critiques in addition to the one on Pure Reason. Nevertheless, for the last 150 years the creativity of man has largely become not a corollary of, but a substitute for, a transcendent principle of order. It has been the tendency of our poets to relinquish, at first reluctantly, then insistently, the transcendent: no ideas but in things! The poets have said: "Thus it is our task to create infinity within these boundaries, for we no longer believe in the unbounded,"[17] which might be Wallace Stevens, meditating the exterior made interior on an ordinary evening in New Haven. It may be indeed that this freedom from the tug of the infinite that has so beset man's past, inspiring not only some of his better but many of his worst moments, will be the truth that shall set us free. This may well be the case for the most sophisticated and authentically modern observers, though some of us are yet tender-minded. We have not learned to live with the situation, to translate all our old transcending metaphors into a new language, and in our stubbornness we may insist on making a better compromise with the older wisdoms. For the new freedom seems to have yielded its own difficulties. If the old beliefs in the transcendent froze men into dogmas, locked them motionless into orthodoxies, then the new immanentism seems to be having trouble finding anywhere to rest, or any means of telling one moment from the next. The principle of the creative intelligence has led to an aesthetic and a life-style of desperate innovation. Is it worse to die with Parmenides or

17. Rilke, *Tuscan Diary.* Quoted by Heller, *The Disinherited Mind,* 162.

Heraclitus, from the inability to move or the inability to cease from moving?

Another alternative, if that is what it is, is paralysis. This may occur when one is caught between the two previous alternatives, unable to accept either and unable to mediate between them. Something like paralysis lays its cold hand on experience in the latest poetry of Robert Lowell. It is a faithful mirror of the world we know, and we wonder whether the paralysis it reflects is necessary. If so, it is certainly fatal.

There is one other alternative, and it is related to the first one, entertained above. Perhaps it is not the *only* other alternative, but it is the last I will mention here, and the only one in which I can personally put much hope. The Christian doctrine of the Incarnation is not the only form of that point of view which says that it was not only possible, but necessary, for man to live between two worlds, but it is certainly the chief example of that doctrine in the Western world. Nor is it the only doctrine which says that both the transcendent principle and the immanent principle are essential, and that man denies either of the terms of this polarity to his own destruction. But it is the only doctrine with which I am acquainted that ties such a point of view to an event in human time and by implication places a tremendous burden upon man to understand history and the manner in which he participates in it. It is impossible, at least for me, to revert to belief in a naïvely anthropomorphic deity or in a world that is valuable only as a sort of tournament field, to be forsaken for better places as soon as the testing is over. But it *is* possible to do some re-thinking of the idea of Incarnation, to ask *what* was incarnated, and into what? I do not believe, with Wallace Stevens and his innumerable commentators, that God and the Imagination are one. But I do believe that it is necessary to think of what is implied in the ancient doctrine of the Holy Spirit, and what its relation may be to the human spirit, and to the very involved question of the role of the imagination in human affairs. While this all may sound naïve and provincial—what have such questions to do with the really desperate questions of our society, or even with writing poetry?—I am convinced that any solutions to such questions must involve these matters. I also realize that these remarks are far more cryptic than I would like them to be. But there is no room to deal adequately with them in an essay of this length, and I want to at least suggest the direction in which it seems to me possible to move.[18]

Before turning to the final section of this essay I want to say that I am very aware of a charge that can be made against me: that in choosing to begin with Arnold, and in spending most of my time on Tate and Lowell, and in making the notion of "tension" into something like *the* central condition of the modern mind, I have not only perpetuated a cliché, but have chosen only one of several possible strands in the fabric of the modern mind and ignored the rest. At first this might well seem to be so. Both Lowell and Tate *do* share the catastrophic, apocalyptic imagination. We

18. I have several times before mentioned the name of Owen Barfield in my notes, and I must do so again. My remarks here at the close of this section, and in the next section, are particularly indebted to Barfield's writing, and especially the final five chapters of his *Saving the Appearances* (London, 1957). I repeat that I do not agree with him at all points by any means (for example: it would grieve him, but I am not ready to accept all of Rudolf Steiner's work—of which I have read only a small portion—at Barfield's high estimate). I have, however, found his works to be nearly inexhaustible in their suggestiveness.

might describe Eliot, or even Yeats, well enough using such terms, but what about Williams? Stevens? Pound? Then, too, Tate and Lowell share the specifically Christian consciousness, aware of its own diminution and possible demise. Even assuming my general manner of viewing Lowell were granted, might it not well be asked whether many other modern writers haven't written Christianity off as a dead option from the beginning?

While I can see the pertinence of this line of questioning, I cannot really acknowledge its force. My response is that "modern" literature and thought is not, in my view, something different from romantic themes and aspirations, but in fact an extension of them (here I differ with J. Hillis Miller; I do not acknowledge an *essential* difference between our situation and that of the Romantics). And I would argue, though I have not the time to do so at length here, that there is something *inherently* apocalyptic about the romantic imagination, and so my choice of Lowell and Tate as touchstones is legitimate enough. Even if we argue, as many have, that the personality is continuously creative and self-created, these very conceptions posit the continuous dissolution of the personality's past. The past recedes first into the unconscious, then into collective memory; and the very process points forward to death, to the dissolution of the personality, the end of the self-creating. And this raises the very conception of an ending, of an apocalypse. A critic like Northrop Frye would likely say to me that I persist in thinking in the dramatic/ironic mode, with all its implied dualities, its resistances and struggles, its grasping after escapes and entrances. Of course I do so, but the argument applies—in a sense even more strongly—to the "desperately triumphant poetic humanism" that Harold Bloom sees as the inevitable legacy of romanticism, emerging in Stevens and Rilke. In the well-known passage from *The Necessary Angel*, Stevens cites Simone Weil, and discusses modern reality as a reality of "decreation." Even as he does so he comments that "the greatest truth we could hope to discover, in whatever field we discovered it, is that man's truth is the final resolution of everything." Even as Stevens denies any final fixity, he borrows the apocalyptic metaphor of final resolution, and sounds like nothing so much as a humanistic E. A. Poe writing a new *Eureka*.

VII

WHEN I began the reading and thinking preliminary to the writing of this essay it was because I, like so many others, found in Robert Lowell's poetry something more than the authority and relevance one finds in even the best poets who are one's contemporaries. The longer I read and thought, the more I became convinced that he shared qualities with Allen Tate, and that these qualities were, for me, inseparable from whatever it was that made Lowell more than usually powerful, in fact, representative of what it meant to be "modern." Even upon making every possible allowance for my own prejudices and special views, this conviction grew, and I set out to describe the "pattern of experience" in the two writers. For one reason or another, I found none of the existing descriptions to my liking, and set out to discover my own. I began to use Tate's critical catchword "tension" as a means of describing what the writers shared, as well as a description of those qualities that made the two, for me, touchstones for recognizing a central quality in the modern mind, and a certain way of facing our human experience. And now, I have discovered that my improvising has brought me to a version of something quite familiar: the postromantic poet, caught between two worlds.

But should the contemporary mind by now not be in the place to transcend some of the dilemmas of the postromantic situation, to get out of its stalemated dualism—self here, world over there, in between the Nothing that waits and waits? That surely depends upon what one means by dualism, and upon the method proposed for avoiding it. I quite agree that the object/subject dualism, with the attendant form of scientific thought that has been so incredibly successful in creating the technology of modern Western society, is in many ways rapidly heading into a dead end. And I believe that in any case the division of experience into isolated compartments of the self and the not-self, thinking subject and unthinking object, is radically false and most destructive. On the other hand I do not believe, as some others do, that the battle has already been won in modern poetry and philosophy and that it has been won by proclaiming that there are no ideas save in things, or that the Self is sufficient. To think in this manner seems to me to do little more than to continue to live in a house built by Western philosophy since Descartes, but with the upper story cut off. And it will not do.

As I have said, others do not agree with me on this point. To speak *briefly* of anyone in this context will surely be to misrepresent his position, but I should mention at least a few of those writers who have recently been concerned with subjects related to my own. An obvious example, as I have already suggested, is J. Hillis Miller. He has written a fine book, *Poets of Reality*, which argues that the classic modern poets have, one after another, struggled their various ways beyond dualism, and that one—William Carlos Williams—spent nearly his entire career as a witness to the fact that the attendant frustration is not the necessary and automatic lot of the modern artist. Morse Peckham has written extensively, arguing that we are, or should be, indeed beyond all these things. In *Beyond the Tragic Vision* he rejoices that Nietzsche finally smashed the transcendental nonsense, that we should recognize with him that "human identity has no ground," that whatever *is* is created only by man's continual renewal of his own identity. And in a recent essay on Gary Snyder in *The Southern Review*, Thomas Parkinson says that in Snyder we see a poet who has finally put Western dualisms quite out of his art (if not quite out of his consciousness). I respect these men, and others who argue similarly[19] (I do not imply that these men have identical arguments). I particularly respect Thomas Parkinson when he says that "a larger and more humble vision of man and cosmos is our only hope" and offers Snyder's work as a "set of new cultural possibilities" that may open our eyes to such a vision. Certainly I sympathize with the attitude and feel as Parkinson (and presumably many others) that the history of Man's outrages committed upon himself and his world has gone just about as far as it can.

I can only once more express my scepticism that we are yet "beyond dualism," "beyond the tragic vis-

19. I have found the work of Geoffrey Hartman particularly interesting in this context, especially *The Unmediated Vision* (New Haven, 1954).

ion," or "beyond" any number of things. I believe that there is indeed a desperate need—I do not use the words lightly—for human consciousness to move out of the stage at which it is now caught, but I believe that most of the task lies ahead of us, and not behind. And, since we are after all living in Western culture in the late twentieth century, I must say that I see little practical hope that the Western mind can eliminate from its nature those antinomies that are so much a part of it. I have said that the subject/object dualism of classical modern epistemology seems radically false to me, but that does not mean that I see much hope that we can so Easternize ourselves as to quite eliminate such a duality—Ezra Pound notwithstanding. The trick is, as Coleridge was never tired of saying, to learn to distinguish without dividing, and to realize that the mind and personality are not and cannot be separated from a brute world "out there," but that they participate in a greater life that permeates all reality. That difficult position in which we are tugged simultaneously toward the comic and the tragic, toward the immanent and the transcendent, is not to be solved merely by denying the relevance or the very existence of one of the poles of the duality. After all, dualities become destructive only when we lose the possibility of relating their poles, when the principle of mediation breaks down and we have no sense of participating in the larger reality that includes the poles.

There can be no doubt that the Western intellect has largely lost any such mediating principle, and the result has been, in the radical sense, incoherence: "Things fall apart; the centre cannot hold; / Mere anarchy is loosed upon the world." If incoherence is the result of a decadent dualism, it is well to remember that a plunge into the immanent, into the ceaseless creativity of the person bounded by—Nothing—is not without its risks, its besetting decadence: indiscrimination. Is it worse to go mad from being unable to place things together ("I can connect nothing with nothing"), or because you can't tell one thing from another; indeed, find it increasingly difficult to speak of things, discover their boundaries wavering? . . . The second alternative looks the more attractive, and certainly more stylish; once in it, who is to say what is madness? We may even decide we have discovered the only blessings yet open to us:

It is a theatre floating through the clouds,
Itself a cloud, although of misted rock
And mountains running like water, wave on wave,

Through waves of light. It is of cloud transformed
To cloud transformed again, idly, the way
A season changes color to no end,

Except the lavishing of itself in change,
As light changes yellow into gold and gold
To its opal elements and fire's delight,

Splashed wide-wise because it likes magnificence
And the solemn pleasures of magnificent space.
The cloud drifts idly through half-thought-of forms. . . .

This is nothing until in a single man contained,
Nothing until this named thing nameless is
And is destroyed. He opens the door of his house

On flames. The scholar of one candle sees
An Arctic effulgence flaring on the frame
Of everything he is. And he feels afraid.
        (Wallace Stevens, "The Auroras of Autumn")

Indeed he does feel afraid, and it is foolish to pretend that he has no reason. And it is foolish to pretend that only the timid scholars of one candle have reason to be

afraid. Hofmannsthal looked in that door, as Hölderlin had before; and so did Rimbaud, and so did Hart
Crane.

For all of their decrepitude and the difficulty they
caused, there was a wisdom contained in all of our
old dualities of body/soul, self/world, immanent/
transcendent, and so on. The man caught between
principles may feel tension. But if you have two principles and some coherent mediation between them—
that is to say, if you have a *polarity* in the true Cole-
ridgean sense of the word—you always have some
place to stand to look at something else, and you have
some justification for using conceptions like "something else." That, basically, is what was worrying Matthew Arnold, and he was at least partially conscious
of it: when you lose the ability to look *at* things, perspective vanishes, the ability to represent external action vanishes. Thus, the suffering in "Empedocles on
Etna" is not only because nature was probably alien
to human concerns:

> Nature, with equal mind,
> Sees all her sons at play;
> Sees man control the wind,
> The wind sweep man away;
> Allows the proudly-riding and the founder'd bark.

There was the corollary fear that anything transcendent impinging on man's experience had been merely
projected by man's own desire:

> So, loath to suffer mute,
> We, peopling the void air,
> Make Gods to whom to impute
> The ills we ought to bear;
> With God and Fate to rail at, suffering easily.

Arnold didn't have the courage to press the question,

and he repudiated his poem. That is the usual position. It is undoubtedly true, for the most part. But one wonders if Arnold may not have known what he was about, if he did not glimpse Empedocles' suffering being transformed, to a degree that even Coleridge in his more clairvoyant moments could not have forecast, into the passionate inwardness and the drunken internal landscapes of the postsymbolist poets.

Almost exactly a century after Arnold's famous Preface we find Allen Tate thinking on what is essentially the same subject. Tate, of course, is looking *back* on what Arnold's subject had become: it is a moot question whether Arnold really prophesied the history of his subject or not. In 1951 we find Tate writing in "The Symbolic Imagination":

> it is the business of the symbolic poet to return to the order of temporal sequence—to *action*. His purpose is to show men experiencing whatever they may be capable of, with as much meaning as he may be able to see in it; but the action comes first. Shall we call this the Poetic Way? It is at any rate the way of the poet, who has got to do his work with the body of this world, whatever that body may look like to him, in his time and place. . . .

The operative word in the passage is, of course, *action*; but immediately related to it are *show* and *see* and *men experiencing*. No one is so naïve as to believe we can resurrect the classical *mimesis*, and certainly Tate is not suggesting this (as Arnold had seemed to a century earlier). One cannot turn back the clock in quite that way. But to *show* and to *see* implies an opposing other force; and it is *men* and their actions that we are attempting to see. Our poetry of the last fifty years has been haunted by "voices," "personae," "consciousnesses," and the like, but there are precious few *people* to be found.[20] A little later in the essay Tate writes:

> Catholic poets have lost, along with their heretical friends, the power to start with the "common thing": they have lost the gift for concrete experience. The abstraction of the modern mind has obscured their way into the natural order. Nature offers to the symbolic poet clearly denotable objects in depth and in the round, which yield the analogies to the higher syntheses. The modern poet rejects the higher synthesis, or tosses it in a vacuum of abstraction. If he looks at nature he spreads the clear visual image in a complex of metaphor, from one katachresis to another through Aristotle's permutations of genus and species.

It is easy to drag out the slogans to refute this: failure of nerve, reactionary, Catholic nonsense, irrelevant to the modern mind. But to say of Tate (or for that matter, of Erich Heller at the close of "The Hazard of Modern Poetry") that this is debating the issues fought out in the nineteenth century is surely to beg the question. Everyone *knows*, or ought to, that after Coleridge, Nietzsche, Kierkegaard, Freud, we can never be the same. The question is, is there only one way we can be?

> Sleep, sleep. The ocean, grinding stones,
> can only speak the present tense;
> nothing will age, nothing will last,
> or take corruption from the past.
> A hand, your hand then! I'm afraid

20. Another statement that can be quarreled with, but it could be documented at tedious length. Naturally the facts are open to argument. Are Prufrock, Stetson, Tiresias, people? For all of the talk, quotation, and citing of documents in the *Cantos*, the structure of the poem is determined finally by the consecutive experience of Pound's mind. In all the length of Stevens' poetry there are no people: many hoots, cries, and whispers; paramours, strange plants and animals, Canon Aspirin—but no people.

to touch the crisp hair on your head—
Monster loved for what you are,
till time, that buries us, lay bare.

Lyndon Johnson once quoted from "Dover Beach," and attributed the lines to a poet he admired very much in spite of the fact that the poet had refused an invitation to the White House: Robert Lowell. I wonder what happened to the speech-writer responsible for that particular bit of "ghost-written rhetoric." Perhaps Mr. Johnson, in addition to his other talents, is a literary critic, for there are things that make less sense than juxtaposing "Dover Beach" and "Near the Ocean." It has now been over a century since Matthew Arnold proclaimed that passive suffering was not a proper subject for poetry—and failed to find any alternative (William Butler Yeats, enunciating the same principle, could at least exclude flagrant offenders from the *Oxford Book of Modern Verse*). Robert Lowell is a better poet than Matthew Arnold was, and he has continued to write; at times it seems as if he writes so much in the hope of proving that Arnold was, after all, wrong.

That is in many ways unfair to Lowell, as has been my whole procedure of using him in a representative and symbolic fashion (there is so much that is so good in his work that I have not even touched on). John Berryman probably made a truer comparison when he once suggested that Lowell was akin to Hölderlin as a poet capable of evoking that moment when things are about to spin out of control, the moment when all seems poised on the edge of desperation. If this is truer of *Life Studies* than some of his later work, it is nevertheless true that Lowell was nearly supreme among contemporary writers in this ability to bring the point just before the breaking point into poetry. That is something of very great value, and I am not sure there is anything in his later poetry, for all of its skill, to replace it.

One of Allen Tate's "Sonnets at Christmas," written in 1942, opens:

> The day's at end and there's nowhere to go,
> Draw to the fire, even this fire is dying

It would take an innocent reader indeed who saw in those lines only the description of the end of a winter day. In two lines, that gets close to the center of the subject, to its essential *feeling*: there's no place to go. And yet there must be some place to go if there is to be poetry, or any other significant action. It would be ludicrous for me to suggest that anyone, let alone a poet of Lowell's stature and character, should change his style or his views or his sensibility. It's absurd to think such things get changed and it is presumptuous for any critic to advise in that manner. One must live his life in the best way he can, and pretend that the days are not as evil as we know they are. Yet, when Lowell writes "O to break loose" one wishes that he could do so. In wishing it, we wish also for ourselves, knowing that if there is any breaking loose it must be into a place where we can *see* and *act* simultaneously, into a vision which, if not of something so large as the whole, is yet more than a point edging into Nothing.